NEEDING THE NANNY

A DADDY NEXT DOOR ROMANCE

MICHELLE LOVE

HOT AND STEAMY ROMANCE

CONTENTS

About the Author	v
Sign Up to Receive Free Books	vii
Blurb	ix
1. Chapter One	1
2. Chapter Two	7
3. Chapter Three	15
4. Chapter Four	22
5. Chapter Five	26
6. Chapter Six	32
7. Chapter Seven	39
8. Chapter Eight	46
9. Chapter Nine	53
10. Chapter Ten	60
11. Chapter Eleven	67
Sign Up to Receive Free Books	73
Preview of No Promises	74
Chapter One	76
Chapter Two	87
Chapter Three	93
Chapter Four	101
Chapter Five	106
Chapter Six	113
Chapter Seven	119
Other Books By This Author	127
About the Author	129

Made in "The United States" by:

Michelle Love

© Copyright 2020 – Michelle Love

ISBN: 978-1-64808-084-5

ALL RIGHTS RESERVED. No part of this publication may be reproduced or transmitted in any form whatsoever, electronic, or mechanical, including photocopying, recording, or by any informational storage or retrieval system without express written, dated and signed permission from the author

❀ Created with Vellum

ABOUT THE AUTHOR

Mrs. Love writes about smart, sexy women and the hot alpha billionaires who love them. She has found her own happily ever after with her dream husband and adorable 6 and 2 year old kids.

Currently, Michelle is hard at work on the next book in the series, and trying to stay off the Internet.

"Thank you for supporting an indie author. Anything you can do, whether it be writing a review, or even simply telling a fellow reader that you enjoyed this. Thanks

Facebook
    facebook.com/HotAndSteamyRomance

Instagram
    instagram.com/michellesromance

SIGN UP TO RECEIVE FREE BOOKS

Sign Up to Receive Free E-Books and Audiobook Codes.

Would you like to read **The Unexpected Nanny, Dirty Little Virgin** and **other romance books** for **free**?

You can sign up to receive these free e-books and audiobooks by typing this link into your browser:

https://www.steamyromance.info/free-books-and-audiobooks-hot-and-steamy/

Or this one:

https://www.steamyromance.info/the-unexpected-nanny-free/

BLURB

My life was perfect as it was, hidden away in my palatial home, unbothered by the world. Until the day it all came screeching to an unpredictable halt.
What did I know about raising babies?
Nothing, that's what.
Moreover, I didn't want to know anything about the subject. The kid on my doorstep wasn't mine and I didn't care what his crazy but absentee mother has to say about it.
But just like the unexpected delivery, which had spun my life on its axis, Troian was just as surprising when she entered my life...

CHAPTER ONE

Troian

"Sammy! Please, I'm begging you, put your shoes on!" I pleaded for what was maybe the sixth time in ten minutes. "We're going to be late!"

I didn't add the word "again," even though it was implied.

"Coral didn't put her shoes on!" Sammy argued, and I rolled my eyes all the way up to the sixteen-foot ceiling, my gaze resting on the intricate wainscoting on the balcony above as I tried to find my patience.

Mr. Thompson peered down at me, a bemused look on his face.

"How's it going down there, Troian?" he teased, and I forced myself to give a smile.

"Great!" I replied with feigned enthusiasm. "We're almost ready to go."

He snickered at my obvious lie as he watched the twins run amok, shooting one another with fake laser guns.

His lighthearted attitude did a lot to help my mood. Even on stressful mornings such as this, I couldn't deny that I was very lucky to be working for a couple like the Thompsons.

"Sammy," I tried again, switching tactics this time. "All your friends are waiting for you at school. You want to see your friends, don't you?"

That seemed to stop the six-year-old for a minute, his blue eyes resting on my exasperated face as he contemplated what I'd said.

"That's true," he agreed, finally hurrying off to oblige my request as I quietly exhaled and turned my attention to his sister.

"Coral? Sammy's putting his shoes on now. Shouldn't you do the same?"

The adorable redhead turned her guileless eyes on me and gave me that sweet smile that always warmed my heart.

"Okay," she replied in her quiet way, heading off to join her willful brother. I exhaled with relief.

I'd already known that if Sammy went, it would be no issue getting Coral to follow suit. After all, I wasn't new to this.

Mr. Thompson broke into a slow clap from his spot on the balcony, a wide grin on his aging face.

"You have it down to a science now," he teased me and I laughed.

"There's a method to everyone's madness," I replied lightly, heading toward the foyer to ensure that Sammy hadn't grown distracted on his quest to find his shoes.

"You certainly have a way with them," Mr. Thompson chuckled, turning to descend the floating staircase and meet us in the entranceway.

Sammy had managed to put his tennis shoes on the wrong

feet while Coral sat primly on the stairs. Ready and waiting, she had her hands folded neatly over the lap of her overalls.

"Let me fix that for you," I told Sammy, but that was easier said than done—of course, he fought me.

"No! This is the way they go!" he insisted, scooting out of my reach. I stifled a sigh, determined not to let my employer see my chagrin.

To my extreme gratitude, his father intervened. "Sammy, if you don't listen to Troian, I'm taking your iPad away."

The boy looked at me balefully, as if I had been the one to utter the empty threat. I knew full well that Mr. Thompson wouldn't follow through; if he was even home this evening, he wasn't likely to remember the punishment. The man traveled on business so much, I was surprised to see him at all.

"Okay," Sammy grumbled, permitting me to adjust his footwear. I glanced at Mr. Thompson with a thankful smile.

"All right!" I cried, happy that the morning ritual had been completed. If we left in the next ten seconds, I might actually get the twins to school on time for once. "Let's go!"

I shuffled them out of the house after they kissed their father goodbye and ushered them toward the minivan, which was mine to use exclusively. It was just one of the many perks of the job at the sprawling, gated mansion in Virginia Beach. Others included a monthly spa package and my own suite, including a fireplace and private bathroom with a Jacuzzi tub. I would've taken the job for the Jacuzzi alone, which I used abusively.

It wasn't a bad gig I had going on with the Thompsons. I'd been with the family for just over a year, and I would do just about anything to keep it going.

Granted, the twins could be a handful at times, but I'd dealt with much worse with my last family. I had no problems with children throwing temper tantrums, but when the parents followed suit I had zero patience. The last house I'd worked at, the single mother had been a diva from the seventh circle of hell and I'd been happy to leave her for the Thompsons.

As I secured the kids in their booster seats and closed the door, a movement caught my eye through the shrubbery separating the Thompson's property from the house next door.

"House" was the wrong word.

The Thompsons lived in a mansion, and that was impressive enough. Ashe Morris lived in a palace—a colossal structure that seemed to span half the beachfront.

I grudgingly admitted that it was a gorgeous piece of property. It was a stunning combination of Greek and Mexican architecture, at least from what I could tell from the brief glances I managed to get from the beach or through the live oaks and Japanese climbing ferns.

Mrs. Thompson had once told me that Ashe Morris had designed the house himself.

From what I'd read online, Morris was a nouveau-riche tech genius. He'd made his first fortune on an app that tracked anything and everything—from a missing set of keys to a kid, and everything in between.

Gone were the days of Amber Alerts and posters for lost pets. With a tap of a finger, a GPS tracker could find that missing tennis shoe hiding under your bed.

Looking toward the motion, I caught a glimpse of his shocking blond hair through the branches. A familiar, embarrassing shiver of warmth shot through me.

I had never said two words to the man, though not for lack of trying on my part. On the occasions where I did manage to catch his bright blue eyes in passing, it was as if he looked right through me. Not that it was surprising, really; I was the hired help, not his peer. Still, a "good morning" greeting every now and then wouldn't have killed him.

It bothered me that I found him so attractive when it was clear that his beauty was only skin-deep.

My eyes can't form an opinion on personality, I reasoned, unintentionally rising on my tiptoes to catch a better look at him. I could just make out the crown of his head, but found myself longing to catch a glimpse of his profile, the arc of his regal cheekbones, or a peek at his full mouth. I would have settled for the bulge of his neck muscles, too, but he had already disappeared from my field of vision.

"Looking for something?"

I gasped and whirled at the sound of Mr. Thompson behind me, my pale skin flushing crimson at being caught.

"No, no!" I cried, my voice sounding just a bit too loud. "I just thought I saw something."

"Something like Ashe Morris?" he asked dryly.

"Oh, of course!" I said, playing dumb. "It must have been the neighbor."

He shook his head and unlocked his Mercedes with the fob.

"You should probably get going," he reminded me. "The kids are going to be late for school."

Embarrassed, I nodded quickly and apologetically. "Yes, sir."

"You know, Troian, you can call me Nathan. And my wife would love it if you'd call her Lisa," he told me, shaking his head as he slipped into the driver's seat.

I did know that. He and Mrs. Thompson had brought it up numerous times, but it didn't feel right—no matter how often they insisted.

They were older than the average parents of six-year-old twins—much older. I wasn't clear if the twins were a result of invitro fertilization or a traditional surrogate, and I dared not ask something so devastatingly personal. Either way, I knew they were both in their sixties. I didn't feel right about calling them by their given names when they were the same age as my own parents—respect your elders and all that.

Of course, I would never say anything like that to their faces, and Mr. Thompson wasn't waiting for a response anyway. He waved to us and drove off, no doubt on his way to close another million-dollar business deal somewhere.

It occurred to me that I hadn't seen his wife that morning. However, that didn't mean much in a house as big as the Thompson's. Mrs. Thompson could have been anywhere in the vast mansion, from the gym to her California king bed—which she did not share with her husband.

The rich are such weird creatures, I thought dryly. I tried to imagine myself as a late middle-aged woman raising two young kids and juggling a career while systemically ignoring her husband.

But none of that was my business. My job was to care for their ginger-haired twins and mind my own affairs, which wasn't difficult to do. I had very little with which to concern myself.

Sammy banged on the window and I snapped to attention. I had wasted more time standing in the driveway in the mounting Virginia sunlight than Sammy had putting on his shoes.

Flipping my shoulder-length blonde hair over my shoulder, I flashed the kids a smile as I opened the driver's side door.

"Ready?" I called, and they nodded in unison.

Time to face the day.

2
CHAPTER TWO

Troian

IT WASN'T REALLY my job to clean up, but I couldn't sit back and do nothing while Emma fussed around the house. The kids were in school so we made a routine of it, even though I'm sure my presence drove Emma crazy.

She had given up asking me to stop "helping" because she realized her pleas were falling on deaf ears. She liked to joke that if I kept helping her then she'd be out of a job, but I wasn't trying to annoy her; I simply didn't do well with idle hands. Besides, I knew being the only housekeeper in a place this size couldn't be easy, so I was happy to help her when I could.

I was in the living room, picking up a pile of toys that the twins had managed to unearth in the short time between waking and leaving for school, when the weather took a turn. The sun outside the long, rectangular windows disappeared, a mass of clouds rolling in like some dark omen.

"You know that we have a housekeeper, right?" Mrs. Thompson asked, shaking her head as she appeared in the entranceway of the open-concept living room. "No offense, Troian, but I think you cause Emma anxiety when you do this. She has a very particular way of doing things, and I'm sure she just redoes it all when you're not looking."

I sighed and lifted my head, smiling wanly.

"I know," I confessed, looking at the refined woman before me. "But I can't help myself. It's been so different since the kids started full days at school. There's only so much Instagram I can handle."

Mrs. Thompson laughed and nodded, stalking toward me in a red, tailored suit.

She was formidable, tall and rigid, as if there was a steel rod in her spine. In all my time working for her, I had never seen her look less than perfect. Her makeup was always subtle but stunning, her short black bob gleaming, without a hair in place. If it was a wig, it was a damned good one, but I found it hard to believe that anyone could manage that kind of gleam with a dye job.

Mrs. Thompson studied me with pensive brown eyes.

"I like you so much more than I liked the last one," she informed me and I grinned to myself. It was something she said often, but I still felt proud every time she said it.

"Thank you, Mrs. Thompson."

"Well, except for that," she scowled. "What will it take to get you to call me Lisa?"

That was the first time I realized that it genuinely bothered her, and I wondered why. Did it make her feel old?

I was contrite.

"I'm sorry ... Lisa," I offered, almost choking on the word as I said it. A grin appeared on her face.

"Now was that so hard?" she chuckled, her face softening

slightly. She didn't look as old as her husband, but I knew they were only a couple years apart. I wondered if she'd had Botox, but again, it was none of my business.

When it came to looks, she couldn't have been more different from her husband. I always found it a little odd that she cared so much about her appearance when her husband didn't seem to care at all.

"You're a good Southern girl, Troian. In some ways, you remind me of myself before I met Nathan."

My brow furrowed, sensing a little wistfulness in her voice. It was incredibly difficult for me to envision Lisa Thompson as a "good Southern girl." She was a shrewd businesswoman, one who lived independently, even with a husband, and strove for perfection.

But who was I to argue?

"Thank you, ma'am," I replied, unsure of how else to respond. I hoped she meant it as a compliment, but sometimes it was hard to tell with her. Her husband was much easier to read, but I found men usually were.

She was staring at me and it was starting to make me uncomfortable. I wondered what was going through that gleaming head of hers, but I didn't need to wait very long to learn what she had in mind.

"I need a favor," she explained. "Well, actually, a friend needs a favor."

"Of course, Mrs.—" I stopped mid-sentence as I caught her death stare. "Lisa. What can I do to help?"

"I'm only suggesting this because you seem to be bored when the kids are in school and, frankly, I'm getting tired of hearing Emma complain about your 'help.' It's ultimately your decision, but I think he would appreciate it, given his circumstance."

I eyed her curiously.

"Who?" I asked, intrigued by this little mystery. "What circumstance?"

"Our neighbor, Ashe Morris. He needs help caring for his young son, and since you're mostly free during the days, I thought you might be interested in taking the job. You would be well compensated for your time, of course."

I gaped at my boss, her words not making much sense.

"His son?" I echoed. Since when did the hot guy next door have a son? I'd never seen a child on the property, or any sign of one. There were no toys or bikes or screaming temper tantrums carrying over from his place. Granted, the walls were thick, and Ashe seemed to value his privacy. But still, hiding a kid back there?

"Yes. I'm not sure what the boy's name is, but he's only eight months old. He's very sweet—"

"An infant?" I choked. "I didn't even know he was married!"

It was an antiquated thing to say, I know, but it was the first thing that flew out of my lips.

"He's not ..." Lisa Thompson looked at me as if I had grown another head. "But I don't believe that's a prerequisite to having a child."

"Of course not!" I said quickly, shaking my straight, honey-blonde hair. "Uh ... what about Sammy and Coral?"

"You will still live here and see them off to school in the mornings and pick them up in the afternoons. On weekends you can bring the baby here, if you want. If you can handle it, that is, and if Ashe wants you on the weekends. We can work it out."

I could not stop staring at her like a deer caught in the headlights. The longer I stood there in silence, the more her brow knit.

"There's no pressure, Troian. If you don't want to—"

"No, I do!" I interrupted before I could stop myself. "You're right. It'll be good for me to do something during the day."

Not to mention that I could use the extra cash. I didn't intend to be a nanny for the rest of my life. I was saving up to go to college and buy a car. Every cent would help me move closer to my goal.

"Excellent. Why don't you go over there right now and see what he needs? I'm not going to lie to you, Troian, Ashe is pretty stress out. He looks like he's about to pop a gasket whenever I see him lately."

I thought she was supposed to be selling me on the idea.

"It's fine," I replied, rising from the faux fur carpeting on the floor. "I dealt with Sammy in the aftermath of his sugar theft, remember? After that, I think I can handle anything."

She laughed and then grimaced at the reminder, shaking her head.

"That boy ..." she sighed.

"I don't know. They say that girls are sweet when they're small but end up giving you the most trouble in the long run."

"Well, lucky me, I get to experience both joys," Lisa chuckled. "Go ahead. I'll call Ashe and let him know you're heading over."

I nodded, feeling my pulse quicken slightly as I rounded the corner and headed toward the front door. Pausing at the mirror, I quickly checked out my reflection to make sure I looked presentable.

My hair was slightly disheveled, but there wasn't too much I could do about that right now. Not when Ashe was expecting me.

My gray eyes shone back at me with their usual impish twinkle. I could never quite figure out why eyes gave off such a look, because I never had a devious thought in my head ... well, not often, anyway. My face was rosy from the sun after spending the weekend with the kids at the beach, and while I wasn't winning any beauty pageants in my Lululemon track suit, my lean, athletic figure looked just fine beneath the pink and white material.

Not exactly job interview material, but it'll have to do, I told myself, hurrying out of the house.

As soon as I stepped foot onto the interlocking drive, a crash of thunder erupted over my head, making me jump almost out of my skin.

I peered up into the sky and wondered how the storm had rolled in so quickly. It had been beautiful and sunny just that morning.

Raindrops began to fall as I rushed through the walkway gate and around the live oaks across the sidewalk. Just beyond, I could see the waves crashing along the shoreline of Virginia Beach as the waters of the Atlantic swelled and families hurried like ants to find shelter. The day had turned on them unexpectedly, and the beachgoers all watched as their belongings got soaked by the sudden storm.

I was drenched by the time I reached Ashe's gate. I jabbed the intercom impatiently, shivering as my T-shirt clung to my frame.

There was no audible response but the wrought iron gate swung inward and I bolted up the driveway. I sprinted the fifty feet to the front door, hoping it would be open and ready for me, but I had to stop and wait under the Roman columns for someone to come.

When no one appeared for a solid minute, I used the lion's head knocker to announce my arrival, feeling slightly irritated. Obviously, someone knew I was there; they had let me inside the gate.

I strained my ears, trying to hear any sounds coming from the other side of the heavy door, tapping my foot as rain streaked from my hair down my back and into my pants.

My teeth were chattering lightly and I was about to knock

again when the door abruptly swung open, causing me to fall forward into the foyer.

Startled, I tried to regain my footing as I slid over the shining marble, looking up at Ashe Morris in surprise. He made no move to help, but instead eyed me up and down with obvious contempt.

"What are you doing here?" he demanded, folding his arms over his broad chest. At his rude words, I finally managed to collect myself, rising to my full height of five-six. He still seemed to loom over me.

"I—" The question had taken me aback. I guess Mrs. Thompson hadn't gotten around to calling after all.

"Mrs. Thompson said you needed some help with your baby?"

His mouth parted slightly and I thought he was going to contradict me. Maybe a part of me hoped he would, because the way he glared at me made me regret agreeing to even speak with him.

"Yeah," he finally agreed, spinning away from the entranceway. I stared after him, unsure if he expected me to follow. I decided it was safest to remain in place.

He stopped just before he disappeared through the hall that presumably led to the right wing of the house and stared at me like I was an idiot.

"Are you coming or what?" he snapped.

Trying to shake off my shock at his aggressive attitude, I nodded quickly and hurried to join him.

"Christ, you're dripping all over the place," he groaned, but he continued down the back hallway.

Suddenly I heard the high, shrill cry of a baby. I looked ahead to see that Mr. Morris was standing in front of the pantry door, waiting for me to catch up.

"He's in there," he told me. "Good luck."

With that, he spun around and walked away.

At first I thought he was kidding, and I stood there like a moron as the baby's cries increased beyond the closet door. But as the pitch reached a deafening tone, I could stand it no longer, and I pushed the closet open to investigate.

Another rumble of thunder seemed to accentuate my movement, as if forewarning me of what I might see. I willed myself not to overreact, telling myself that I wasn't living in a horror movie and therefore shouldn't expect anything horrific.

I exhaled with relief when I realized that I was neither standing in a pantry, nor was the child alone. The room served as a guest room, or maybe a staff bedroom, and the boy was wrapped in the arms of the housekeeper. The poor woman was trying to silence him with coos and a singsong tone, but she looked exhausted.

I looked over my shoulder, fully expecting Ashe to appear with a smirk on his face, but he was nowhere to be seen.

He had just left me, a total stranger whose name he probably didn't even know, to take care of his baby boy.

What kind of asshole would do something like that?

CHAPTER THREE

Ashe

No matter where I went in the house, the kid's cries echoed in my ears. It was impossible, of course. The walls were too thick for that, and the distance between my office and my housekeeper Cynthia's on the main floor was too large for sound to travel that clearly.

There was only one explanation as to why I might be able to hear the infant, even after jamming earplugs in my ears. It wasn't a thought I wanted to dwell on.

My frustration was growing. I had to get out of there, but before I could consider moving from my high back leather chair, there was a knock on my office door.

"What?" I snapped.

Cynthia poked her head in, her eyes narrowed. "Your nanny is going home. She has to pick up the Thompson kids."

"Why are you telling me this?" I demanded.

Cynthia grunted, as if I should already know the answer to my own question. "I guess that means you're not going to tend to your son then?" she replied caustically, and I felt shivers slide up and down my arms.

"He's not my son! Stop calling him that!"

"Well, he sure as hell isn't mine, Ashe, and I don't know how I got stuck with babysitting duties!"

Our eyes clashed but in true Cyndi form, she didn't falter.

"I have a nanny for the daytime now," I answered through clenched teeth. Kids that age slept all night, didn't they? What more did she want me to do?

"Ashe, it's been three days. His mother is nowhere to be found. You can't just toss him around like he's a football—"

"Cynthia, I already told you I'd pay you double for this. What else do you want from me?"

"I want you to spend some time with Will! He's a sweet little—"

"I have work to do," I interrupted coldly. "Close the door behind you."

Of course, she didn't move, but instead folded her arms over her ample chest in disgust.

"You're gonna need a better plan than this, Ashe," she warned. "What if Collette doesn't come back?"

"Of course that con artist will be back," I snorted. "She thinks she's walking into a major payday."

"Ashe—"

"Cyndi, get out!" I roared, rising angrily and placing my hands firmly on my desk. Calling up the glare I used when negotiating million-dollar business deals, I stared her down for all I was worth. Finally she relented, spinning to leave me alone in the office with my thoughts.

I knew I was being unreasonable, especially toward her. After all, it wasn't Cyndi's fault that my ex had dropped her infant son off on my doorstep three days earlier and then disappeared without a trace.

When I'd answered the door that day, the last thing I'd been expecting was to be greeted by a helpless infant.

All she had left was a note pinned to the child, with some horseshit written on it about the baby being mine. I'd barely read it.

"That kid is not mine!" I'd growled hotly, staring at the chubby-cheeked infant.

He hadn't seemed to care about my anger though, and had simply puckered his wet lips and eyed me with stunningly blue eyes. He looked nothing like me, and the math was all wrong anyway ... wasn't it?

I couldn't think straight in my fury, grabbing my cell phone from the back pocket of my jeans and scrolling through my contacts for my ex's number. Of course, it was disconnected when I called it, which simply made me angrier.

I whipped the cell against the floor, the sickening sound of the screen cracking only adding to my roiling emotions.

On cue, the baby began to cry.

"Oh, Ashe, you need to calm down," Cyndi chided me, scooping the kid from his car seat. "Babies are sensitive. They pick up on moods."

"Call Child Protective Services and get this kid out of my house," I yelled. The child wailed louder and my head began to pound.

"You're not thinking," Cyndi snapped, rocking the unsettled baby in her plump, strong arms. Her porcine face contorted with worry and she shook her head.

"How the hell can I think when someone's just left a baby on my doorstep?" I yelled. "Screw this. You take him. I'm calling CPS."

"Ashe, don't!" my housekeeper yelled and I found myself freezing in mid-step.

Cynthia had been with me since the beginning. I'd met her when my family was renting a small bedroom in a house in Richmond, my family hardly having a pot to piss in or two cents to rub together.

She'd also lived there at the time, and she'd picked up extra cash from the landlord for cleaning up after all the tenants. We'd become friends pretty quickly, especially after she decided to take pity on me by bringing me sandwiches and candy to keep me sustained.

I'd always known I was going to design something great, my aptitude for computers having started back before I could talk.

Actually, that's not true. I could talk; I'd just chosen not to until I was almost five. And Cyndi had been my only support during that time.

I owed her a lot, and when I'd finally cashed in on all my potential, I'd brought her with me—though she'd insisted on earning her keep.

She was more than a housekeeper to me, and she had her own suite and bathroom. She made her own schedule and she had full run of the house. Somehow, she always managed to keep the fifteen-thousand-square-foot mansion in pristine condition. I secretly suspected that she hired a cleaning crew when I was out of town, but that was none of my business.

I liked having her around. She was like the older sister I'd never had, but that also meant she knew how to get under my skin like no one I'd ever known.

I could hear the ice in her voice, and I waited.

"What if he is yours, Ashe?" she asked. "Look at his eyes. They certainly look like yours."

I swallowed the lump in my throat because I'd had precisely the same thought. But I wasn't willing to just accept that.

"He's not," I said flatly. "He can't be."

"You don't sound convinced," she replied softly.

I turned to look into his eyes. "He's not," I insisted flatly. "I'm calling CPS."

"And if, by some chance, he happens to be yours, Ashe, do you really want CPS involved? Do you know the kind of mess that could create?"

I felt my back tense. I didn't need a reminder about how CPS operated. I had very nearly ended up in the system myself several times when I was kid.

I probably would have been better off if I had been put into foster care, I thought, eyeing the kid as if justifying why I would call.

But ultimately, I knew that Cyndi was right. I couldn't do that, not until I knew for sure if he was mine.

But holy hell! I did not want to be a father, and certainly not if Collette Patrick was the mother. That woman was a walking train wreck.

"You deal with him," I told Cyndi in the end. "I can't deal with this."

That had been three days ago and I was no closer to tracking down Collette. The woman had disappeared off the face of the earth.

There was a knock on the office door and I looked up, surprised to see Cyndi again. I could tell she wasn't alone.

"Who else is here?" I demanded as the door swung inward tentatively. To my surprise, the neighbor's nanny stood in the doorway. What was her name again?

"Troian. I thought you went to pick up the twins."

"I'm leaving now," she said quietly. "And I'm sorry to interrupt, but I was just wondering if you want me to come back tomorrow after I take the Thompson kids to school."

She and Cyndi stared at me expectantly, and I found myself meeting her slate-gray eyes for the first time.

I'd seen her dozens of times in passing. I'd have to be blind not to notice a pretty blonde with long legs and an eternal golden tan, but she was young. And the neighbor's nanny. So, off limits, pretty much.

Sure, I'd checked her out when she wasn't looking. No red-blooded male could resist watching her tiny, perfectly round ass as she bent over to secure the kids in the car, or peering at her perky, firm cleavage as she lounged around the pool in a bikini.

But I had never gotten close enough to look her in the eyes. Better to stay away from temptation, I'd always thought. However, now that she was right in front of me, I was stunned to realize how lovely her irises were.

Obviously she had more than just a sexy body.

I wrenched my gaze from hers, a foreign sense of embarrassment sweeping up through the back of my neck, knowing that I'd stared at her too long.

"Ashe!" Cyndi growled. "She's waiting for an answer."

"I don't care what you do," I muttered, turning my attention back to the computer screen. Cyndi exhaled and pulled Troian out of my office.

"If you could come tomorrow, you'd be doing me a huge favor," I heard her say to the girl as the door closed. "Don't mind Ashe. He's very busy with work."

Work was the least of my concerns at that moment. I sat back, steepling my hands and willing myself to be calm.

I had procrastinated on the matter long enough. I had to figure out what to do with this baby, since it was clear his mother had abandoned him.

Again, my ears filled with the sound of low, plaintive wailing, and I groaned to myself. I buried my face in my hands.

But oddly, when my eyes closed, it wasn't baby Will's face that lingered in my mind.

Instead, I saw a pair of mischievous gray eyes smiling back at me.

I shifted uncomfortably in my chair, trying to adjust the new tightness I was experiencing in my crotch.

Oh no, you don't! I yelled at myself. *Hands off the babysitter.*

CHAPTER FOUR

Troian

As I drove the twins home from school, my mind was anywhere but on their mindless chatter as they chirped about their day.

Usually, it was my favorite part of the afternoon. I loved bonding with them and asking them questions about what they'd done and who they'd talked to. Listening to little kids' chatter was just about the most entertaining thing I could ever hope to be doing, and the twins never failed to amuse me.

But that day, I couldn't tear my mind away from baby Will and his wretched father.

How can he treat an infant like that and where the hell is Will's mother? I wondered. *What kind of mother leaves their baby with a man who has no interest in being a dad?*

Cynthia had been great, walking me through the makeshift routine she had started with Will over the past few days. And while I was dying to ask questions about what I'd walked into, I kept my mouth shut.

I'd been working with wealthy families long enough to know that asking questions was a big no-no. I was on a need-to-know basis, and it was clear that in Will's case, I didn't need to know anything but how to change a diaper.

It had only taken me five minutes to calm him down, and Cynthia had been awed by my ability to do it so quickly.

"You have a way with babies!"

"I guess so," I replied, snuggling the warm bundle to my body. He smelled so sweet.

"He's what, eight, nine months old?"

"Uh ..." Cyndi looked embarrassed and looked down. "Something like that."

I narrowed my eyes but didn't comment on her lack of knowledge about her boss' son.

Cyndi and I had spoken many times since I'd started working for the Thompson's, unlike me and Ashe. She was a friendly woman with a warm smile, and while she was a little on the heavy side, she was quite attractive.

When Mrs. Thompson had originally told me about the baby, I had wondered if Cyndi was the mother. She was the only woman I had ever seen at the Morris house. But it became obvious very quickly that she wasn't.

"It's nice of you to agree to help," she told me. "Lisa said she wasn't sure if you'd be up for it."

It all made sense then. Mrs. Thompson hadn't spoken to Ashe at all, she had spoken to Cyndi.

"Are you kidding?" I replied lightly. "Have you smelled this kid?"

"Troian, you're not listening to us!" Sammy complained, knocking me out of my daydream.

"Of course, I am. I'm listening very carefully."

"Then what did I just say?"

I hated being outsmarted by children. It made me feel dumb. Lucky for me, I knew there were only a handful of subjects that Sammy usually brought up.

"You were talking about playing soccer with Ben and Billy," I said.

"You were listening!" he cried and I exhaled, glancing at him in the rearview mirror.

I shouldn't be so distracted while spending time with the twins, especially while driving. They were my real job, my main priority, not some self-centered jerk who hid his kid in a maid's room with his housekeeper.

How many bedrooms are in that mansion anyway? Twelve? Fifteen? And he couldn't put his child in a nicer place than that?

My fingers were clenching the steering wheel, my knuckles growing white as I pulled up to the Thompson house.

The gate was open at Ashe's place and I wondered if Will's mother was there. The curiosity was burning a hole in my gut.

Mrs. Thompson's car was in the driveway and the kids flew from the van into the house to find her. Instead of rushing after them as I normally would, I lingered on the drive, peering over the shrubbery for a glimpse of what was going on. Unfortunately, my attempt at sleuthing didn't reveal anything. I didn't see anyone.

It was just odd to see the gate open, as if Ashe was expecting someone. Or maybe I was just reading too much into it.

"Looking for something?"

I yelped and spun, my face flushing bright red as I looked at Mrs. Thompson.

"I—no!" I gasped. "I—"

I didn't even know how to explain what the heck I'd been doing. This was not the kind of neighborhood where spying and nosiness might be tolerated.

"You know, you can just go over there and knock on the door now," she chuckled. "You don't have to check out Ashe from a distance anymore."

I thought my chin might hit the floor.

"What?" I gasped. "I—I don't check out Mr. Morris!"

"Sure you do," Lisa replied, unlocking her car door. She reached into the passenger side to retrieve some file folders before grinning at me.

"Oh, don't look so shocked, Troian. You're a beautiful girl, and he's a sexy older man. It's a tale as old as time."

"Mrs. Thompson!" I choked. "Please stop!"

"Suit yourself," she giggled. "But if you don't act on it, maybe I will."

She winked at me and disappeared into the house, leaving my gut twisting in a dozen different ways.

She's just kidding. She's a married woman! She's sixty! He's not interested in Mrs. Thompson. He's at least twenty years younger than she is, without a wrinkle on him. I could hardly stop staring at his rippling arms as he leaned over the desk to look at me.

Suddenly, I was confused.

Why did I care what Mrs. Thompson did with Ashe? He was a world-class jerk and a terrible father.

And if Mrs. Thompson would cheat on her husband with him, then maybe they deserve each other.

I turned back and stormed into the house to collect the twins. I had to distract myself before I let the question fully form in my mind and humiliate me further.

But it was too late.

If I don't care what they do, then why am I so angry?

CHAPTER FIVE

Ashe

I SWIRLED the spoon around in my bowl, eyeing the cornflakes as they sank deeper into the bowl of milk.

I wasn't hungry, but I knew I had to eat something. I didn't deal well with hunger, and I knew if I missed breakfast then I'd be miserable all day. Even if I ate an early lunch, I'd be off. There was nothing to do but force the soggy mess into my stomach and get back upstairs to work.

It was a quirk, but it was one of the more minor ones I'd acquired over the years. Maybe that was why I was still single—too many quirks.

Yeah, that's the only reason. Women can't handle your endearing quirks.

I took another spoonful of slop and pushed the bowl away. It was all I could take. If that meant my day was going to go downhill, so be it. I'd had so many shitty days this week, what was one more?

I was nearly finished developing the software for another app, one that would probably piss off a lot of people, but who cared about being PC anyway? If you weren't doing anything wrong, then you wouldn't have to worry that your significant other was tracking you without your knowledge, right?

Okay, so that marketing strategy might not fly, but marketing was not my game; technology was.

I rose from the stool at the marble island and dropped the bowl into the sink. Before I could steal up the back stairwell, I heard a tinkling giggle flow through the hallway.

I turned instinctively and cocked my head toward the sound, a slight shiver flowing through me.

It was the nanny, of course. Cyndi sure as hell didn't laugh like that. But what was she laughing at?

I padded across the kitchen floor, my Adidas shoes moving soundlessly over the hardwood floors, and looked out toward the foyer.

"You are the best boy, aren't you? Aren't you?" the blonde cooed, leaning over the stroller, using her index finger to poke the baby's nose playfully.

Suddenly I heard what had made her laugh so sweetly. The second her fingertip made contact, the child burst into peals of laughter, deep chuckles straight from his belly. The sound was cartoonish and hilarious, and although I couldn't see his face, I could envision what his chubby little cheeks looked like in that instant.

I froze in my little hiding spot, watching as Troian exploded into another round of chuckles, her smile almost blinding.

"Who's the best boy? You are!"

They howled like two drunken teenagers, and I found myself grinning in spite of myself too.

"Who's the best—aw, Will, did you just poo?"

I let loose an unexpected gust of laughter, slapping my hand over my mouth and ducking back into the kitchen as the nanny looked up.

"Hello?" she called. "Cyndi?"

Ah, shit!

I heard her voice moving closer as she asked again, "Cyndi, are you here?"

I rushed toward the back stairs, hoping to make my escape before she realized I had been watching her. I knew there wasn't enough time.

Instead, I snatched my cell off the counter and pressed it to my ear just as she entered.

"Cyn—oh."

"And I don't care how long it takes!" I yelled into my phone as if I was having a heated conversation, pretending I didn't see her standing there.

Through my peripheral vision, I saw her turn to leave. With her walking away, I suddenly felt incredibly foolish.

Why had I acted like that? Like some stupid kid avoiding his high school crush? Or like I'd been doing something I shouldn't have done? I was a grown-ass man in my own house, yet I was sneaking around on eggshells.

Enough was enough.

I threw the cell back onto the counter and strode out into the foyer, where she was gathering Will in her arms. They must've just returned from a walk or something.

"Hey," I said as she moved toward the staircase.

She glanced over her shoulder.

"Oh, hi," she said. There was no warmth in her voice, but her gaze told a different story. Did I see her eyes rake over my bare arms and tank-top-covered chest?

"Let's just get something straight. This is my house," I spat. "You're an employee, and not even one I hired. I don't need you skulking around, listening in on my conversations." The words felt wrong as soon as they left my lips, but I'd already started down this path.

Her dark blonde brows knit together and she studied me warily, her eyes focused on my face now.

"I am aware of that," she replied slowly. She seemed to hold Will closer to her body, angling him slightly away from me. The next words died on my lips.

Why was she holding the baby like that? Was she afraid of me? Did she think I would hurt the baby?

The idea was preposterous. I wasn't scary. I might be a little loud sometimes, maybe a bit brash, but I definitely wasn't someone to be feared.

"I didn't know you were in the kitchen," she offered when the silence became awkward. "I thought you were Cyndi."

I nodded slowly, my eyes lowering. I couldn't quite identify the sensation flowing through me. Was it ... guilt? Shame?

My gaze slid up toward the baby and he cooed at me, those bright blue eyes fixated directly on me.

"Is there anything else?"

Troian's voice carried like pellets of ice shooting me in the face, but I couldn't find my own to reply.

To save face, or at least what I thought was saving face, I shook my head and whirled away as if I'd had the last word.

But as I sauntered up the back stairs, my mind whirling slightly, I tried to make sense of what had just happened there.

Why had I faltered when I wanted to tell her to stay out of sight? It was my house and I wasn't going to let Collette's stupid plan, no matter what it was, screw up the home I had created for myself.

This will all be over soon, I assured myself as I walked into my office. *I have the DNA kit coming in the next couple days. Either Collette will show up and collect her son, or the moment of truth will send the boy to CPS. Either way, I'll be free of this invisible restraint sooner or later. Until then, I just have to put up with this disruption in my life.*

I should have felt better about that, but I didn't for some reason.

The sound of Troian and Will's laughter echoed through my head, but it was cut off by the memory of the nanny's look of concern. She had been worried about the baby, maybe even for herself.

I would never hurt anyone! I thought furiously, pounding my fist against the desk in anger. *I'm not my stepdad.*

My hand was throbbing from the impact and I looked at myself in the mirror above my desk, shaking my head.

I needed to get my solitary life back, once and for all. I didn't need a kid or a beautiful, pixie-eyed girl upsetting my balance. There were plenty of women around if I needed one, no matter what my crotch was thinking.

Pushing thoughts of Troian out of my mind, an even more disturbing train of thought took over. The blue of Will's eyes flooded my memory and I flopped back into my chair, willing myself to think clearly, to focus on one subject at a time.

Could the kid really be mine? Had I been too hasty in dismissing him?

The blond peach fuzz on his head was beginning to show the same golden hue as mine. True, Collette was a blonde too, but she wasn't as blonde as I.

I rose from the desk, suddenly unable to sit still, and wandered toward the window overlooking the backyard.

Unbelievably, Troian and the baby were in the backyard by the pool, talking to Cyndi while she tended to the gardens. How could that be, when I had just seen her going upstairs? Had she gone outside to avoid me? It was entirely plausible.

She's everywhere, that woman, I thought in annoyance, but I didn't turn away. Just as I had in the hallway, I sat back slightly and peered at them from a distance, noting the way the sunlight glinted off Troian's golden strands.

She had slipped on a tank top over her bathing suit, her bronzed arms glistening as if she'd just applied sunscreen. I wondered if she was going for a swim, looking to the baby as he stared adoringly at her from a blanket near the edge of the pool.

She held one of his hands as she continued to chat with Cyndi, her head moving gracefully to display the lines of her lean neck. Watching the way she moved, I was seized by the irresistible urge to run down there and sink my lips against the curve where her neck met her shoulders.

What would she do if I snuck up behind her and kissed her, cupping my hands over her perky little tits and tweaking those nipples, which I know are dying to escape her bikini top? Would she slap my face? Or would she let me do it?

My erection touched the wall and I moaned slightly, slipping my hand around it, biting my lower lip.

"Down, boy," I muttered to myself. "You've got enough problems as it is. No need to create more."

But it seemed that my words had less and less effect on my aching member. He seemed to be vying for control, and something told me that my logic was not going to get in the way of his desire.

CHAPTER SIX

Troian

AFTER OUR STRANGE encounter in the kitchen, I started to notice Ashe staring at me when he thought I couldn't see him. He'd lurk in the shadows of the house, as if he was trying to catch me making off with the silver candlesticks in the dining room.

If he didn't trust me in his house, why didn't he just find someone new to watch Will? Why did he continue to stare at me with those brilliant blue eyes? He always looked at me with wariness and ... what else was it I read in his glowering expression? It was difficult to pinpoint, but sometimes I swore it was lust. And it filled me with heat from head to toe.

The thought that he might replace me filled me with panic, though. I had grown so attached to the little boy and his infectious laughter over the past week. I wasn't any closer to learning about his mother, although I had tried to broach the subject a couple times with Cynthia. She immediately shut me down every time. She was loyal to Ashe, a sealed vault when it came to whatever secrets lurked behind the walls of the Morris mansion.

Every day, after I sent the twins off to school, I rushed over to be with Will. When the weather was good, I took him in the stroller to the beach or the park, trying to avoid the tension that Ashe seemed to cause with his very presence. But if I'd given it any thought, I'd have noticed that I took a little extra attention with my appearance in the mornings now.

I'd even started putting on mascara, something that Lisa Thompson commented on one morning as I started next door.

"Aren't you all dolled up for babysitting," she taunted me, and I turned back to look at her.

"What do you mean?"

"I don't think I've ever seen you wear makeup when caring for the twins."

I blushed furiously and cursed myself for it. I didn't want her to read the embarrassment in my face.

"I have," I replied defensively.

"How's it going over there, anyway? I keep meaning to ask Cyndi if Ashe got the results back yet."

I blinked in confusion. "The results?"

She eyed me and pursed her lips together.

"It's none of my business," she said quickly, reaching for her car keys. "And it's certainly none of yours."

She was gone before I could ask her another question, not that I thought she would give me any answers anyway, but I felt an unexpected stab of worry at her words.

Was Ashe sick? Was that why he acted so coldly towards everyone? Was it cancer? Something worse?

A dozen bad thoughts flooded through my mind as I made my way toward the house, quietly slipping in through the back doors. Every morning I walked into the house that way, into the kitchen where I expected to find Cyndi feeding Will his breakfast.

To my absolute shock, Ashe was leaning over the baby in his high chair, speaking to him in a low voice.

He hadn't heard me come in yet, and I watched in awe, stunned to see him so close to the boy.

What was he doing?

Goose bumps prickled over my arms as I tried to make sense of what I was seeing. I had never seen him so close to Will and it made me apprehensive.

Straining my ears, I tried to hear what he was saying, but I couldn't quite make out the words. All of a sudden, Will threw his head back and began to howl, his little face red with rage.

"What are you doing!" I yelled, striding toward the highchair. Ashe spun and looked at me in surprise.

"Nothing!" he replied defensively as I shoved past him to pick up Will. "I was ... I was just talking to him."

I scoffed, cuddling the baby to my chest. "You haven't said a single word to him since I've been here and suddenly you're talking to him? What did you say to make him cry?"

I knew I had no right to speak to Ashe like that. Even aside from the fact that I knew Will didn't understand any mean or bullying words Ashe might've said to him, Ashe was Will's father, and he might even be dying. But my maternal instinct had kicked in, and all the anger I'd felt toward him over the past week had reached a tipping point as Will sobbed in my arms.

"I ..." he seemed confused by the question. He stared at me, his eyes darkening as I continued to shush Will.

Without answering, he turned and spun from the kitchen, his chiseled jaw tightening in anger.

"It's okay, Will," I cooed at him. "Everything is fine. Have you had breakfast yet?"

He seemed to calm down as I put him back in his chair and found him some pureed peaches for breakfast.

The second the spoon touched his puckered mouth, his mood lifted and he was back to his babbling self.

He'd just been hungry. Shit. I'd already felt bad for my overreaction to Ashe's presence, and this just made me feel worse.

"Oh! Don't tell me Ashe left the baby alone!" Cyndi cried, hurrying into the kitchen with two paper grocery bags in hand. "I left him alone for five minutes!"

I shook my head quickly.

"No, he was here when I came in," I replied, exhaling slowly.

"I just had to run to the store for diapers. Will's in his last one and we both know how fast he'll go through that."

I forced a laugh I wasn't feeling, a sense of guilt tickling my gut.

Had Ashe finally been sharing a moment with his son, and I'd ruined it with my suspicions? It certainly appeared that way.

"Are you okay?" Cyndi asked, and I realized I had spaced out for a minute.

"Yeah, I'm good," I replied quickly, turning my attention back to the baby. I was silent for a few minutes, making silly faces at Will, but there was a question weighing heavily on my mind.

Finally, I blurted it out. "What test result is Mr. Morris waiting on?"

I didn't look at Cyndi directly, pretending to be fixated on Will's bright eyes, but I could feel her stare burning into the back of my head.

"Who told you anything about test results?" she demanded after a moment. It didn't take an expert to note the concern in her voice. Lisa had been onto something.

"Is he sick?" I murmured softly, my eyes darting toward the doorway. I didn't want him to overhear me asking questions about him, questions that I had no right to ask. But the mystery was becoming too much to bear, and the more time I spent with Will, the more I knew I needed the truth about his parents. Both of them.

"Troian, I like you," Cyndi said shortly. "I think you're a nice girl, and you've helped us out a lot."

I wasn't stupid, I knew what that meant. I waited for the caveat.

"But Ashe is your employer and you should know better than to ask questions about his personal life."

I swallowed down the emotion in my throat, knowing that she was right, but unwilling to let it go.

If Cyndi wouldn't tell me, I would have to learn the truth another way. She had already spoken to Lisa about it. Maybe I could find a way to get the twins' mother to disclose whatever she knew.

Will's well-being is my concern, I told myself, but I also knew that was just a weak justification for my nosiness.

I was deeply bothered by the thought that Ashe might be ill. He seemed so impenetrable, so strong. How many times had I envisioned my legs wrapped around his broad waist, his rock-hard abs pressed to my flat stomach?

Too many.

The idea that he might lose that power, the muscles—even his forbidding presence—in the aftermath of an illness? It was heartbreaking. What would happen to Will?

My imagination was running amok, and it must have shown on my face as I stared off into nothingness, my heart thumping with sadness.

Just when he seems to be coming around. Maybe that's why he's coming around. He's making peace with his son before he dies.

"You need to wipe that look off your face." Cyndi grumbled, rolling her eyes as she approached the glass table where I sat feeding Will.

"I'm sorry," I mumbled. "I was just ... thinking."

"You were making up silly tales in your head," Cyndi corrected with exasperation. "I could read it all over that innocent little mug of yours."

"No!" I protested weakly, but she grinned.

"I'll tell you what's going on but you have to keep your mouth shut. This really is absolutely none of your business, but I think it's fair that you understand what's happening. I just don't think that Ashe would agree."

I lifted my head to stare at her wide eyes, nodding enthusiastically.

"I promise!" I vowed. "The secret is safe with me."

She nodded slowly and sighed, sinking into the chair beside me.

"There's a reason that Ashe has been so cold toward Will," she explained, and I cocked my head to the side. A quick flash of him leaning over to whisper to his son crossed my mind.

"Why? Is he dying?" I asked before I could stop myself.

"Dying? Of course not," she laughed. "The devil doesn't want Ashe."

She chuckled, but I wondered if there wasn't some truth to her words. Still, I was consumed with an immeasurable feeling of relief to learn he wasn't sick after all.

"No," Cyndi continued. "Ashe is being so standoffish because he's not convinced Will is his son."

My eyes bugged.

"What?" I demanded. "Why?"

"That is a long story, and I'm not about to get into all the details, but he has good reason. You can't fault him for not wanting to get attached to a kid who might not be his in the end."

I bobbed my head slowly, understanding it all with blinding clarity.

"So you need to cut him a little bit of slack, okay, Troian?"

"Yes," I replied, sitting back to stare at Will, the corners of my mouth twitching slightly.

He'd have to be blind not to see the resemblance between him and this baby, I thought as Cyndi rose from the table to finish her morning routine.

But I knew Ashe wasn't blind. He was always watchful of everything around him, examining the world with those intense teal eyes.

He was coming around, slowly but surely.

I had witnessed it myself.

My shoulders sagged as I exhaled the breath I'd been holding. I'd been hasty in judging Ashe. He'd had his reasons for behaving as he had.

And I owed him an apology for what had happened. I just hoped he would accept it.

I would simply have to find a way to present it to him in a way he couldn't refuse.

CHAPTER SEVEN

she

I MADE my way down the front stairs, noting that the house was silent. I hadn't seen Troian and Will by the pool like they'd normally be just after noon, so I assumed they had gone to the beach.

The house felt empty without the sound of baby coos echoing through the halls, and while I would never admit it aloud, I longed for the giggles of my son.

My son. Shit. When did I start acknowledging that he belongs to me?

Who was I kidding? I had been sneaking in every night to watch him sleep in his nursery on the main floor, often sitting with him for hours when my insomnia was at its peak.

He would crawl around on the office floor in the evenings when Cyndi was otherwise engaged, and I had finally gotten him to laugh the way Troian did by pretending to play dead on the floor.

Babies are so morbid, I thought affectionately, pushing my way into the library. I needed a specific book to finish my work, and I was ninety percent certain I had a copy of it in my personal collection.

If not, I'd need to check out Amazon.

I started when I saw Troian sitting in the room, her long legs draped over the arm of a wing chair, her shoulder-length hair cascading over the swell of her V-neck T-shirt.

She heard me enter and quickly sat up, dropping her legs to the floor as if she'd been caught in a compromising position, her hands folding over the book in her lap.

"Oh, Mr. Morris," she gasped. "I—I'm sorry. I was just reading."

Her cheeks stained a pretty pink as she stood up.

"Where's Will?" I asked, my eyes scanning the room for a glimpse of the baby, but he was obviously not there.

"Napping. He always naps at this time."

I nodded slowly, stepping toward her as she gazed at me with nervous eyes.

"I'll get out of your way," she told me, moving to brush past, but I stopped her instantly, my hand grasping the soft flesh of her upper arm.

As if my hand was made of ice, her skin exploded into a rash of gooseflesh and her pupils constricted as she looked at me.

"You don't need to go anywhere." I meant the invitation to be an olive branch, of a sort, but my voice came out much huskier than intended, bringing a new meaning to the words.

Our gazes locked and the electricity buzzing between us was tangible. I felt the heat emanating off her body, and I couldn't stop my eyes from raking over her face and across that delectable neck of hers. I saw her nipples pebble through the flimsy material of her shirt, and my eyes caught there for a moment. Was she wearing a bra?

I was going to find out in a second, but I just needed to be sure. I was eager to get the go-ahead signal I'd been yearning for.

She lifted her head to look up at me fully, her gray eyes the color of summer rain clouds. Her mouth parted slowly, her breaths quickening as if she could see the events that were about to transpire playing behind her eyelids like a movie.

"Are you afraid of me?" I asked gruffly, not releasing her arm.

"No ..." she whispered, but it wasn't a ringing endorsement.

Why did the fact that she might be afraid of me send a surge of heat into my crotch? It made my desire to possess her even more powerful. I knew I would never hurt her, but the uncertainty in her eyes was a driving force behind what I did next.

I pulled her toward me, my mouth inches from hers, our eyes still engaged.

"I'm going to kiss you," I told her. She nodded, her pink tongue lolling out to wet her lower lip in anticipation.

I brought my mouth down, crushing my lips to hers, and she tried to gasp from the impact. My tongue jutted forward to touch the tip of hers, my fingers tightening against her arm as I whirled her forward to face me fully.

I watched as her lids grew heavier until they closed entirely. Snaking my other arm around her waist, I yanked her into me, wanting her to feel the rush of heat in my shaft.

Troian sighed deeply and I nuzzled her cheek, my hand moving down to cup the firmness of her ass. She bucked forward slightly and even through the material separating us, I felt the heat of her core.

I wanted to taste her, every inch of her. Her flesh was already proving to be the honey I had anticipated, and I knew it would only get sweeter the lower I got.

Abruptly, I pulled back, pushing her down into the armchair

she'd been occupying just moments before. She fell gracefully, her slender thighs parting easily.

"Take off your shirt," I growled and she nodded. I could see she was trembling as she lifted her top over her head. I groaned, my hands automatically reaching for the taut nipples I had been thinking about more and more lately.

She hadn't been wearing a bra.

I buried my face in her chest, inhaling the coconut scent of her skin as I pulled down the waistband of her shorts.

They slid off easily, exposing her creamy cleft, and I threw the clothing over my shoulders, followed by her calves.

I pulled her forward, my palms spreading her cheeks from underneath as my lips found her bellybutton.

Troian's fingers entwined in my hair and she pushed me lower, a low moan escaping her lips. Arching her back, she urged me down, and I could smell her sweetness even before my tongue lapped at the already pulsating button.

"Mm," I murmured, my lips flush against her. "You're soaked."

She shivered, another round of goose bumps erupting on her flesh, and I dove into her, my tongue exploring every crevice of her core.

Troian yelped, her hands tightening over my blonde head, her hips moving rhythmically against my steady licks.

Every taste made her wetter and my eyes darted up to look at her without losing my groove. She seemed to be floating above herself—there, but not there. Her tongue lolled out of her mouth and she mewled loudly, bucking up unexpectedly so hard, she likely bruised my mouth. Still, I didn't stop, clenching her ass to keep her in place as she tensed.

"I—I'm cumming!" she cried, and satisfaction filled me as her words were closely followed by a stream of heat against my face.

I continued to lap at her, relishing her little thrusts upward until she finally began to relax and settle back to earth.

But I wasn't finished with her, not yet.

Slowly, I raised my mouth over her belly again, my face drenched in her juices. I allowed her to lower her legs to the floor, moving my waist up to meet hers as I pushed my pants to the floor, boxers tangled within.

Our faces just inches apart, I stared at her, watching her dazed eyes widen further as the tip of my shaft teased her swollen nub.

"Oh my God," she mumbled, twitching slightly as I rubbed my tumescent member over her most sensitive spot.

"Do you want it?" I whispered, and she nodded eagerly.

"Oh God, yes," she moaned. "Please."

I smiled, pushing her thighs apart. With no further warning, I jammed my engorged cock inside her, savoring the sound of her screams.

"Oh shit!" she gasped, nails digging into my shoulders for support. "You're huge!"

I filled her entirely, feeling the walls of her center lock around me, and I stifled a groan. I was too excited. I had wanted her for too long. But I couldn't stop, not now, not when I had her exactly where I needed her: begging for more as she squirmed beneath me.

Troian's legs lifted again, this time to wrap around my waist. With her lower limbs holding me tightly, I plunged into her with swift, full movements.

She gasped, disbelief clouding her eyes, and my sac tightened as it slapped at her clenching ass cheeks with every thrust.

I couldn't hold out much longer. Actually, I couldn't hold out at all, but I wanted to feel Troian orgasm around my unit before I exploded.

I closed my eyes, willing myself to hold off, but it was an exercise in futility; I needed release.

As I exploded inside her, my jaw tensed and Troian shrieked, clenching at me furiously. It was only then that I realized she was cumming again.

I held fast to her slim waist as she squeezed every drop out of me, her calves clinging to my back under her crossed ankles.

Our breaths were ragged but somehow matched in their unevenness, and I finally allowed myself to slip out of her, studying her face intently as I did.

Was there any regret there? Any second thoughts?

Before I could open my mouth to ask any of the questions that were popping through my head, Will began to fuss through the baby monitor.

Instantly, Troian jumped to attention. Even through my haze of satisfaction, I was impressed by how quickly she was able to find her clothes. Will hadn't even started crying yet and she was fully dressed, glancing at me apologetically.

"Sorry," she said. "I should go give him his lunch before he becomes inconsolable."

I nodded, reaching for my pants.

"That's a good idea," I agreed. "Why don't you grab him and I'll take you both out for lunch on the beach?"

Her jaw parted.

"Uh ... yeah, of course," she mumbled, clearly stunned by the invitation. "I—I'll just get him ready."

I slipped on my pants and followed her out of the study.

"I'll help you," I told her, and she glanced at me in shock, thankfully making no other comment.

She had every reason to look at me like that. I hadn't exactly been the model father to Will, but if the past few days had taught me anything, it was that tiny babies could bring forth a lot of enjoyment. I didn't need a DNA test to know that Will was my son. Collette wouldn't have left the child with someone she wasn't sure was his father, no matter how wacky she was.

I had been fighting a connection with my own son, and he didn't deserve that. And besides, it was an impossible fight. If Collette never came back, I would be happy to raise the baby on my own.

Well, not all alone. I'll have Cyndi helping.

I watched as Troian picked up the half-asleep infant from his crib and laid him on the change table, making teasing sounds at him as Will peered at her affectionately.

Looking at her taking care of my son, I felt a strange tug at my heartstrings. *Shit.* Looked like my son wasn't the only person I'd bonded with against my best efforts, no matter how foolish those efforts might've been. I had inadvertently developed feelings for the nanny, too, but for some reason, that didn't bother me as much as I thought it should.

In fact, as I stood there watching them together, I suddenly realized there was very little I wanted more than to keep Troian with us.

I wonder how the Thompsons are going to feel about that, I thought wryly.

CHAPTER EIGHT

Troian

AFTER OUR HEATED encounter in the library, our lives seemed to do an incredible one-hundred-and-eighty-degree turn.

Even Cyndi was shocked at how attentive Ashe seemed to be toward Will. What I wasn't sure of was whether or not she suspected that Ashe and I had been using Will's naptimes for afternoon delights of our own.

Every night after the twins went to bed and I was sure that the Thompsons wouldn't be looking for me, I would inevitably slip back over to Ashe's house. Sometimes I'd stay there until the wee hours of the morning before finally sneaking back home before the twins woke up again.

We weren't exactly being discreet, but we didn't go out of our way to flaunt our newfound relationship either.

However, Cyndi was a smart woman. She'd probably figured it out, but as she had instructed me what felt like a lifetime ago, she didn't get involved with the comings and goings of her employer.

Lisa Thompson, though, was another story.

"What is going on with you and Ashe Morris?" she demanded one night as I slipped down the stairs. I hadn't realized that she was still on the main floor, and I froze in my tracks at the sound of her voice.

I gaped at her, unsure of how to answer the question.

Ashe and I hadn't discussed what we would tell people, but I knew instinctively that telling my employers that I was engaging in an affair with my other employer would not look good.

"What do you mean?" I asked, shifting my eyes away so she wouldn't read the blatant guilt on my face.

"He's asking if you can work for him full-time now."

I stared at her in shock. That was not something we had discussed. I should have been annoyed that he'd asked her without clearing it with me first, but I couldn't deny that I felt a smidgen of pleasure that he'd thought about it.

"Well?" Lisa snapped. "What do you have to say about this?"

I thought quickly.

"Honestly, he never asked me," I told her truthfully. "But I can understand why he might feel he needs a full-time nanny. I think Cyndi's already dealing with more than she can handle."

My boss's brown eyes narrowed and she looked me over as if seeing me for the first time.

"Hmm," she replied. "Why do I get the impression that there's more to the story than that?"

"I don't know what you mean," I said quickly.

"What are you doing down here?" she asked and I tensed.

"I was just going out to Starbucks," I lied. "Want anything?"

A cold smile formed on her lips.

"No, thank you. But maybe you should ask Ashe if he wants anything before you go though."

She brushed past me and headed up the stairs, leaving me with the feeling that I'd just been caught with my hand in the cookie jar.

I should just tell her the truth, I thought, but I didn't want to go that route. Not yet.

The last week had been going so smoothly at the Morris house, and while I didn't doubt that Ashe was into me, I couldn't guarantee that things would work out.

I certainly wasn't about to move into his house as his employee while we were lovers. Maybe I could split my time better between the Thompsons and Ashe, though.

Why did I feel like I was being pulled in two opposite directions? We all had the same goal, didn't we? Taking care of the kids.

The twins' routine had remained the same and, on the weekends, I brought Will with me to the Thompsons to play with Sammy and Coral.

Maybe Lisa is mad because the twins keep asking for a sibling now that they've met Will, I thought, making my way outside toward Ashe's estate.

I thought I could feel eyes watching me as I snuck through the walkway, but I didn't bother to turn around and look. I had nothing to hide, not really. The Thompsons might not like the idea of me dating Ashe, but I still took damned good care of their children.

"Hey, babe," Ashe called when I walked into the foyer. "I just ordered Thai food. You hungry?"

"A little," I agreed. "Did you talk to Mrs. Thompson about having me come here full-time?"

He looked at me in surprise.

"It's sort of the next step, isn't it?" he asked. "Moving in together?"

His tone was teasing, but I thought I saw a hint of wistfulness in his eyes.

"I don't think she's happy about you trying to poach me," I explained, following him into the living room. "Don't forget, she pimped me out to you in the first place."

Ashe scowled at the word.

"Don't say that," he growled. "And yes, I remember that she offered your services, but according to Cyndi, that's because you were driving her housekeeper crazy during the day. I could have hired my own nanny if Cyndi didn't want to look after Will."

I pursed my lips together and studied his handsome profile. Instinctively, I reached out to touch the line of his jaw, turning his head toward me for a kiss.

It seemed almost impossible to keep my hands off him, now that I had free rein, and I didn't want to miss an opportunity to take advantage of the privilege.

"You don't waste any time, do you?" he teased, stepping into me. I raised my head for a kiss and the now-familiar chills flooded my body as his mouth touched mine.

I didn't know what it was about him that made me melt on contact. Perhaps it was the fact that I had followed him with my eyes for over a year, yearning to know what he felt like beneath his shirt.

He joked with me, but the heat of his groin against my thigh told me I had exactly the same effect on him.

I sighed deeply, feeling his hand curl into my hair and yank my head to the side to allow for his kisses.

He latched on, sucking against the soft skin of my throat. I struggled to get away, knowing he would leave a hickey—again.

But that was part of his game. He liked marking me and making me squirm, and I'd have been lying if I said I didn't love it too.

"You are such trouble," I grunted. As the words left my lips, he spun me around without warning, bending me over the back of the sofa.

My mini-skirt rose over the line of my ass, his left hand easily sweeping between my thighs.

"Already wet," he purred. "Right on schedule."

I was pinned against the cool leather as his hands continued to explore my center, fingertips probing at the dampness, sliding under my panties and slipping back and forth until his index finger rested on my throbbing button.

Groaning, I tried to watch him over my shoulder but his grip tensed in my hair, pushing my face against the red leather cushions so he could work me some more.

A familiar tingle mounted in my belly and I danced on the edge of an orgasm. But I knew I would never get there, not like that.

He knew that too, but it didn't stop Ashe from continuing the pleasurable torture of manipulating my clit, building my excitement as I begged him for release.

"Please!" I moaned. "Why do you torture me?"

"You are just so delicious," was his response. "I love to keep you in limbo, pleading for more."

I wondered if his touch would ever lose its novelty, but I doubted it. Not when I turned into butter with even the slightest contact.

For several minutes, I twisted under his grasp, bucking my heated cheeks back against him, trying to encourage him inside me.

I moaned and panted, a line of sweat forming on my brow, but he wasn't relenting. Ashe was determined to make me wriggle like a worm on a hook.

"Oh, baby, please ..."

Two fingers slipped inside me without warning and I cried out at the suddenness of the motion, but I knew he was going to finish me, finally. His digits probed me, feeling my slick core as he brought me toward my climax, his thumb rubbing the sensitive skin of my clit.

"Cum for me now," he ordered. I did not need a second command.

A hot gush flowed from me and I mewled, my knees knocking against the back of the sofa.

He finished me easily, withdrawing his hands from my crotch and releasing my hair as I gasped with pleasure.

I watched him over my shoulder, his eyes locking on mine as he licked his drenched fingers, one by one.

"Fuck me," I whispered, but as I said the words, the intercom buzzed.

He shrugged nonchalantly, spinning away.

"Sorry. Food's here," he said flippantly. I gaped after him, wondering how he could simply walk away from me splayed out like this when I knew he had to be sporting a raging hard-on.

I shook my head in disbelief, rising up awkwardly to straighten myself before the delivery man showed up at the door.

I could smell the scent of me filling the room and I was instantly embarrassed.

I hoped Cynthia wasn't home. I hadn't exactly been quiet.

Well, I reasoned, *if she's home and didn't know about us before, she definitely does now.*

Ashe reappeared with the takeout in his hands.

"Let's eat this in the kitchen," he suggested. "In case Will wakes up."

I nodded, and followed him toward the back of the house, pausing to look in on the baby as he set up the food.

"Hi, little guy," I cooed, stroking his cheek softly as he slept. Babies always looked like cherubs when they were asleep. I could watch Will all night, his sweet mouth parted and moving slightly, as if he was suckling on his soother.

Would it be so bad to move in here full-time and take care of him? It would certainly be easier than doing it from the Thompson's, and the twins certainly didn't need me as much as Will did.

Reluctantly, I turned away to leave him under his mobile and joined Ashe in the kitchen.

"I've made a decision," I said as I entered.

"Oh yeah? What's that?" he asked, searching through the drawers for some utensils.

"I'm willing to move in here full-time to take care of Will."

Ashe stopped what he was doing and looked at me, a slow smile forming on his lips.

"Oh, you silly girl," he laughed. "I didn't want you to move in here to take care of Will."

I blinked, a hot flush of humiliation flooding my face.

"Oh," I muttered. "I—I thought—"

"I wanted you to move in here to take care of me," he cut me off, his grin widening.

I exhaled with relief. "Oh, I'll take care of you, all right," I replied, laughing.

CHAPTER NINE

Troian

IN THE LIGHT OF DAY, maybe my decision to stay with Ashe wasn't the best. I'd made it while I was sexually charged and not thinking clearly, and I hadn't really thought about how I was going to tell the Thompsons.

I knew that it wasn't going to go over very well, but it had to be done. After I dropped the twins at school, I returned home instead of going directly to Ashe's house.

Lisa wasn't home, but Nathan was, and I counted myself lucky. Of the two, he was probably the more reasonable, but who could really say?

"Troian! Shouldn't you be next door?" Mr. Thompson asked as I knocked on the door of his study.

"I'm going in a minute," I told him. "But I need to discuss something with you and Mrs. Thompson first. Is she going to be home tonight?"

"Oh, she didn't tell you? She's in New York until next weekend, and I'm off to Seattle for three days. It's just you and the kids starting tomorrow. Is everything okay? Can you just talk to me?"

Shit.

"Oh, okay," I said, turning to leave. "No, everything is fine. It can wait."

"Are you sure?" he called after me, but I nodded.

"Of course."

"Troian."

I turned back to him reluctantly. "Yes?"

"I think I know what this is about," he said slowly. "And I have to say, I don't think it's a very good idea."

I swallowed a reply as I stared at him.

"Troian, you're a grown woman, and you can make your own choices," he continued, and I grew tenser with each word he spoke. "But I fear you're not thinking with the right organ in this matter."

"Mr. Thompson, I'm not sure what you think I wanted to discuss, but I assure you, it's nothing to worry about."

"Troian, if you want to change jobs, that's none of my business. Obviously, Sammy and Coral adore you, and we would be very unhappy to see you go, but that is ultimately your choice. But if you're doing it because—"

"I'm not changing jobs!" I interrupted in a panic. The last thing I wanted was for the Thompsons to think I was leaving them. I had invested over a year of my life into their household.

Mr. Thompson's brow furrowed in confusion.

"Oh!" he said. "I thought you were leaving us to move into Morris' household." I shook my head vehemently.

"That's not what I wanted to talk about," I lied.

"Oh. Well, pardon me for being so presumptuous. I should

have known you were much too smart to leave a good job to go chasing after a man you hardly know."

I frowned.

"With all due respect, Mr. Thompson, I am twenty-one years old. I can make adult decisions about who I date."

"I agree," he replied, throwing his hands up in mock surrender. "But you should probably be better informed about a man before you move into his house, wouldn't you agree?"

I didn't know what to say. Was he trying to warn me about Ashe in some convoluted way, or was he just speaking as a concerned employer?

I didn't ask because I didn't want to have that conversation with Nathan Thompson. I was sure my cheeks were already crimson with embarrassment.

Forcing a smile, I shrugged my slim shoulders.

"Well, like I said, that wasn't what I wanted to talk about. Have a good day, Mr. Thompson."

I was gone before he could say anything else. As I hurried through the house, I realized that my hands were shaking.

Was there anything to worry about? How could I know? I knew so little about Ashe Morris, except that it felt so right to be with him.

But Mr. Thompson is right. There's no need to rush into this.

It really could wait. For weeks I had been dividing my time between the two households. But as Ashe had said the other day, it wasn't like the move was only about watching Will.

Most nights, in fact, it was Ashe who got up if Will woke. He was the one who fed the baby breakfast in the morning, and he even changed diapers.

"I don't know what you need me for," I sighed. "You've got this down to a science."

"You know exactly why I need you," he retorted, his voice gruff. It was that tone that sent shivers through my body every time. I loved it when he growled in my ear when we were making love.

The move will keep, I thought, making my way over to the house with a skip in my step, like some lovestruck teenager. *And Ashe won't force the issue if he thinks I'm not ready.*

"Good morning!" I chirped as I opened the French doors into the kitchen. "Where are my favorite men?"

I was met with silence, so I padded toward Will's room, my ears honed for signs of life in the house.

"Hello?"

I pushed open the door to the nursery. It was empty.

"Ashe? Cyndi?"

A weird feeling of dread tickled my belly as I continued through the hall. I headed toward the front entranceway but I still saw no one.

Was there a doctor's appointment I had forgotten about? It didn't seem likely. I was a nanny for a reason. I could remember scheduled appointments without effort.

I glanced out the front door and saw that the car Ashe usually drove was in the driveway, morning dew still touching the hood of his Mercedes.

"Hello?"

I reasoned that Ashe must've taken Will up into his suite while he got ready. Cyndi was probably at the store.

I climbed the stairs toward the second floor, but as I approached the closed bedroom door, I heard nothing.

"Ashe?"

I pushed open the door to the bedroom. The sitting room was empty but the television mounted on the wall was on, albeit on mute.

"Ashe?"

"Yeah."

His voice startled me and I hurried through the front room and up the few steps to the bedroom.

Ashe was lying on the bed, staring up at the ceiling blankly. A single sheet of paper lay at his side.

"Are you sick? What's going on?" I demanded. "Where's Will?"

He didn't answer and I slid onto the bed beside him, peering worriedly at his face. He was unusually pale.

"Ashe!" I snapped, pushing his face toward me. "Where is Will? What's wrong?"

He smiled at me, but there was not a single trace of mirth or humor in it.

"He's gone."

My blood turned to ice chips.

"What do you mean 'gone?'" I demanded, leaping from the bed. "His mother came for him?"

He chuckled. "No one knows where she went, and I think it's pretty clear she's not coming back for him."

"I don't understand!" I yelled. "Where has he gone?"

Fear tickled my stomach. Had he done something to Will?

I shoved the wicked thought out of my mind and tried to focus on what he was saying.

"Where did he go?" I asked again, a pleading note in my voice. "Please, tell me what's going on."

He didn't reply but he tossed the paper laying at his side at me. I snatched it up, wondering what it could possibly say.

I stared at it uncomprehendingly. "What the hell is this, Ashe? Please talk to me!" I was becoming hysterical, his deadpan expression alarming me in the worst way.

The sheet was from a lab. The markers meant nothing to me as I tried to make sense of it.

"It's the DNA test I sent away for," he sighed. "Will isn't my kid, Troian."

I felt like someone had knocked the wind completely out of my gut, and I bit on my lower lip as a sob threatened to escape.

"Oh my God ..."

I sank back beside him on the bed, where he remained on his back.

"When did you get this?" I asked. "This morning?"

"Last night."

Shame washed over me. It was the first night in weeks that I had not gone to him, opting instead to catch up on some much-needed sleep.

I should have been here. Of all the nights not to come ...

"Why didn't you call me?" I whispered, curling up beside him. To my utter shock and bewilderment, he pushed me away.

"Why?" he laughed, turning his back to me. "What could you do?"

"I could have been here for you!" I retorted, sitting up. "Where is Will now?"

"I called CPS to come and get him."

Just when I thought I had reached the pinnacle of shock ...

"You what?" I choked. "Why? Why would you do that?"

Suddenly, Ashe sat up and glowered at me, his face contorted into a mask of fury.

"Didn't you just fucking hear what I said, Troian? He's not my kid!"

"I know but—"

"I've had that baby here for weeks and he belongs to someone else! It's kidnapping, Troian. I had to!"

"It's not kidnapping," I whispered, tears brimming in my eyes. "His mother left Will with you."

"And now I'm leaving the kid with CPS."

I was speechless, my head swimming with anger and denial that he would do this. But at the same time, what choice did he really have?

"Get out, Troian. I want to be alone," he muttered.

"No!" I cried. "I'm not leaving you alone."

"You are!" he snapped back, his eyes flashing with malice. "I don't want you here."

The words stung but I gulped back my protests, knowing that he was in far more pain than anything he could inflict on me.

"Ashe—"

"Did you not hear me?" he snarled. "I don't need you here, Troian. I have no use for a nanny anymore. Get out of here and don't come back."

Aghast, I gawked at him. But he ignored me, falling back onto the bed and deliberately turning his back to me, dismissing me entirely.

Gnawing on my lower lip, I backed out of the bedroom. I didn't allow my tears to fall until I hit the sitting room.

He just needs time to process what's happened, I told myself. *He'll call me when he's ready, and we'll get through this together.*

But as I ran from his house, my face streaked with tears, I wondered if that was true.

He had finally let his guard down and let Will into his life. He'd let me into his life, had learned how to love his son—and me as well—and now that child was gone.

How could we hope to survive this?

CHAPTER TEN

THE DAYS FLOATED by after Will was taken away, one melting into the next. My investors were calling nonstop about the app, but I didn't have the drive to work. If not for Cyndi, I probably wouldn't have eaten either.

Troian called a lot in the first few days, but even her calls tapered off.

I wasn't being fair to her and I knew it, but I couldn't do anything to change it. The problem was, I couldn't think of Troian without thinking about Will. I had gotten to know them together, as if they were the perfect little family, hand-delivered to me to make up for my own shitty childhood.

Without Will, it was impossible to look at Troian. The pain was just too great.

"You have to stop beating yourself up," Cyndi told me softly.

"There was no way you could have known. He looked exactly like—"

"I don't want to talk about it, Cynthia. Close the door on your way out."

She grimaced but stood her ground. "At least take a shower, Ashe. You stink."

I scowled at her suggestion. Who the hell did I need to take a shower for? Troian? Will?

I lay in bed for a solid week before I finally snapped out of it long enough to take Cyndi's advice and shower.

I almost felt human again when I emerged, but my heart was broken in so many ways. A simple shower couldn't fix that.

I knew I should at least call Troian, but even the thought of hearing her voice was too much. I couldn't bring myself to do it.

I would eventually ... or at least that was what I told myself. But first I had to cope with the devastation of losing a child who was not even mine to begin with.

"Oh good. You're done moping," Cyndi called when she saw me. "Come and eat lunch."

She gestured at the kitchen island and I reluctantly shuffled toward it, sitting on the stool.

"What are you going to do now?" she asked as she riffled through the fridge, looking for ingredients to make a sandwich.

"Do?" I echoed. "About what?"

"Are you going to call CPS and find out what the hell has happened to your son since they picked him up?"

I bristled.

"He's not my son!" I roared, and she eyed me with naked disdain.

"You are such a child, you know that? No wonder you fell for the nanny—you need someone to take care of you."

I gaped at her.

"I am not a child!" I snapped. "I am stating the facts. Will is not my child!"

"Sharing DNA doesn't make him your kid, you complete dumbass," she sighed. "Waking up in the middle of the night with him makes you a dad. Doing that stupid Gangnam Style dance over and over just to get him to laugh? That's being a dad. You're so hung up on DNA, you don't even know what it means to be a dad. You're the only dad that kid has ever had."

I ground my teeth together, feeling a familiar burning behind my eyelids.

"I'm not the one who's hung up on DNA. I can't just keep a kid because someone left him here. He has a real dad out there somewhere."

"No," she agreed. "But you can at least call and find out what the hell happened to him. See if he's been returned to his parents or if he's floating around the foster care system somewhere."

I inhaled sharply.

What would happen to Will if Collette wasn't found? Or if she was found and deemed unfit? Would he just get tossed around the system?

It made me sick to think that he might fall through the cracks and become just another forgotten child. Not when I had so much to give him here.

"I'll make the call," I said suddenly, jumping from the stool and reaching for the cordless phone.

Cyndi was right. Will was not my biological son, but he was as much a part of me as my own heart.

And if I could find a way to get Will back to me, maybe I could get my sense of family back—not only with him, but with Troian also.

"What the hell are you waiting for?" Cyndi barked at me. "Make the damned call!"

It took me a month to find out everything I needed to know about Will's whereabouts.

I found out pretty quickly that he had been moved out of Virginia Beach. Waiting on phone calls to learn more was one of the worst things I'd ever experienced in my life.

But when I was finally put in touch with his caseworker in Richmond, I learned the heartbreaking news that he had not been reunited with his parents.

"Collette Martin seems to have disappeared off the radar completely," Susan Collins, Will's caseworker, explained through the phone. "I have reports that she was heavily into drugs, so we don't anticipate a good outcome. The child's father is still unknown, however ..."

I waited, my spine so tense I thought it would snap in two.

"... you are listed as the father on the birth certificate, Mr. Morris."

I confess, I didn't know what that meant at first.

"But I'm not Will's biological father," I explained, sighing.

"No," she agreed. "But the fact that you are listed as his father does give you rights as a legal guardian."

Hot, cold, lukewarm, all the sensations I could imagine smothered me in that moment.

"What are you saying? Are you saying that I can have him back?" I choked. "He can come home?"

"If you're willing to take him, yes."

"Yes!" I screamed into the phone. "Yes! Send him home! Where can I get him?"

"Well, I still need to come out and do an evaluation of your home," she explained. "But I don't think there will be any problems, Mr. Morris."

"Schedule it! I want my son back!" I cried, my heart

hammering so loudly, I was sure she could hear it through the phone.

She chuckled dryly. "I'm glad to hear you say that, Mr. Morris. In my line of work, we don't get to see happy endings very often."

After I ended the call, I sat at my desk, willing my nerves to settle down.

I sent Cynthia a text.

Will is coming home.

Her response came just seconds later.

Really? That's amazing, Ashe!

The caseworker needs to assess the house, but he's really coming, I sent off.

There was a pause but I could see that she was writing something, the three bubbles indicating a message was forthcoming.

Isn't there someone else you should be sharing this news with?

I stared at the message for a long time, but I didn't move. She was right; Troian deserved to know what was going on.

I hadn't even caught a glimpse of her outside in the past three weeks. I thought she might've been avoiding me on purpose, and honestly, I was a little glad that she'd done that. That didn't mean that I wasn't filled with loneliness—I longed to be with her every night.

I missed her terribly and I wanted nothing more than to tell her I'd been a fool for cutting her out. But I'd stopped myself, worried that I would just break her heart again if I found myself overwhelmed with melancholy.

But now I didn't need to worry. Our family was going to be reunited again.

Will she forgive me after all this time?

There was only one way to find out.

I pushed back my office chair and raced down the center stairs and out into the bright southern sunshine.

It felt like a day for renewals, for fresh starts. The sun was going to wash away all the gloom and sadness that had filled the halls of the mansion. All the stolen laughter was about to be replaced.

I rang the intercom at the Thompson's place and waited, glancing at my watch.

It was eleven o'clock and I could see that the minivan was parked in the circle drive near the front door.

"Hello?"

"Lisa? It's Ashe Morris."

There was a long pause.

"Hello, Ashe. Is everything all right?"

"Yes! For the first time in a long time," I replied honestly. "Is Troian home?"

There was another, longer silence.

"Lisa? Are you still there?"

"I'm here, Ashe, but Troian isn't."

"Oh. When will she be back?"

Dead pause.

"Lisa?"

"She's not coming back, Ashe. She left two weeks ago."

I paled.

"What? Where did she go?" I demanded. "Did she leave a forwarding address?"

"No ..." The way she said it made me believe she might know something.

"Lisa, please tell me what you know. It's important."

A huge sigh crackled over the intercom.

"I think she went home to her parents in Norfolk."

"Thanks, Lisa," I murmured, turning away.

I was too late. I had been stubborn and stupid and let her go, and now she was gone for good.

Will and I wouldn't be a true family without Troian. I had to find her.

CHAPTER ELEVEN

Troian

THERE IS nothing more humiliating to a grown woman than crawling back to her parents with her tail between her legs. Unfortunately, I didn't have much of a choice in the matter.

My mom was thrilled to see me, while my dad met me with his "I told you so" face.

"See? You should have just gone to college like we told you," Dad declared, eyeing me from over his newspaper. "Look at you, you've gotten lazy. You haven't been exercising, have you?"

"Rob, leave her alone!" my mom scowled, throwing her arms around my shoulders. "You look healthy, sweetie. Your cheeks are pink and glowing."

I felt like shit, but it was a feeling I'd gotten used to over the past six weeks. Being kicked to the curb like yesterday's trash was not a good feeling, especially when I'd known all along that Ashe Morris was a jerk.

My weakness had caused me to lose my job, had set me way back on my path toward my goal, and had obliterated my own self-respect.

Even knowing all that, I still longed for Will's infectious baby giggles, and Ashe's hard body against mine.

I hated myself for missing him.

You don't miss him, I reminded myself. *You miss the guy you thought he was. Ashe Morris is not someone you should miss.*

But when I closed my eyes, I could see the intensity of his blue eyes staring back at me, burning holes through me as if he could see clean into my soul.

I'd been home for two weeks when Mom started getting antsy. It was to be expected, and I couldn't sit around the cottage-style house forever, pretending that the world outside didn't exist.

"So ... honey," she asked sweetly. "What are you planning to do, now that you're home?"

I smirked at her from my spot on the rocking chair where I'd been reading a James Patterson novel.

"Is that your way of asking me when I'm leaving?"

Mom looked horrified at the thought.

"No! I am so glad you're back! You can stay as long as you want," she assured me. I knew she meant it, even if Dad would happily have left me at the circus at the first opportunity.

"I'm just wondering if you have any plans. Do you have enough saved up for college now?"

The sardonic grin on my face widened.

"Oh, I have enough for college," I told her. "But I'm not going to be using it for college."

Her brow furrowed in confusion.

"Why not?"

"Because, Mom, I'm—"

"Troian?"

My head whipped to the side.

Am I hallucinating?

"Oh, is this a friend of yours, honey?" Mom asked, smiling warmly at Ashe as he approached. "Hi, I'm Maddy Carpenter, Troian's mom."

"Hello, Mrs. Carpenter. Ashe Morris."

I watched in disbelief as they shook hands.

"Ashe, what are you doing here?" I demanded nervously. "You shouldn't be here."

"Yes, I should be."

I glanced at my mom, who was beaming like a simpleton at the handsome stranger on her front porch.

"Mom, can you give us a minute?" I sighed.

"Sure! I'll bring you some homemade sweet tea. I think I've got some cookies too."

"Great. Thanks, Mom," I muttered, watching her disappear through the screen door.

"What are you doing here?" I demanded. "Please leave, Ashe. I have nothing to say to you."

Not anymore. It was far too late.

I couldn't go crawling back to him after a month and a half of silence, not now. I would never trust him again. Didn't he know that I'd lost Will too? Was he that selfish?

"I'm an asshole," Ashe said.

Well, that was a start.

I stared at him, my gray eyes narrowing.

"Go on."

He grinned at me sheepishly.

"Will is coming home," he explained. "I've been trying to hunt him down since ... well, for a while."

"Since you told me you didn't need a nanny anymore? Are you here because you need a nanny again?"

My tone was cold, but I was elated by the news. Not a day

had gone by that I didn't worry about the baby, and now I knew he was where he belonged.

"No, I'm here because I need my family back together."

The words filled me with an unexpected wave of affection and longing, and I found myself softening in spite of myself.

"I was so hurt," Ashe sighed. "So hurt. I didn't even leave my room for a week."

The pain in his voice was palpable, and I lowered my eyes, knowing I didn't want to get sucked into this. But the desolation in his words ...

"I couldn't bear the thought of looking at you, Troian. It was selfish and wrong, but I was devastated ..."

He exhaled deeply. "I don't expect you to forgive me, but I did need to find you and tell you that I am sorry for how we left things. You and Will are the closest thing to a family I've ever had in my life and I would do anything to save that."

I raised my eyes and nodded slowly, chewing on my lower lip.

"Why did you leave the Thompsons?" he asked when I still didn't speak. "I was shocked you were gone. Was it because of me, Troian? Because you shouldn't have to give up your job because of me."

"Well, I did," I replied flatly.

He shook his head ruefully and I rose slowly from the rocker, my book falling to the floor.

"I'm sorry," he mumbled as I approached. "I made a mess out of everything. Go back to the Thompsons and I promise you, I won't bother you. I—"

"Stop talking," I instructed, clasping his hands and sliding them over my waist.

"But Troian, we need to talk this through—"

"I had to leave because I'm pregnant with your child, Ashe."

I heard the crash of silver behind me and realized my mom

had been listening at the doorway, but I didn't care. I didn't tear my eyes away from Ashe's shocked face.

"What?" he gasped. "You are?"

I nodded slowly, placing his palms over my still-flat belly.

"Is there room for one more in our family?" I breathed, suddenly feeling unaccountably shy.

"Hell, yes!" he howled, lifting me off my feet and swinging me around until I squealed.

"Troian Grace Carpenter, can you please come inside for a moment?" my mother gasped from behind me. I swallowed a smile. Ashe put me on my feet and we grinned at each other.

"I better deal with the fallout," I said.

"Hey," he called as I turned away to deal with my mom.

"Hm?"

"I love you."

I nodded slowly, my eyes shining.

"I love you," I replied, and I meant it.

THE END.

SIGN UP TO RECEIVE FREE BOOKS

Sign Up to Receive Free E-Books and Audiobook Codes.

Would you like to read **The Unexpected Nanny, Dirty Little Virgin** and **other romance books** for **free**?

You can sign up to receive these free e-books and audiobooks by typing this link into your browser:

https://www.steamyromance.info/free-books-and-audiobooks-hot-and-steamy/

Or this one:

https://www.steamyromance.info/the-unexpected-nanny-free/

PREVIEW OF NO PROMISES

A Bad Boy Billionaire Romance

By Michelle love

∾

Blurb

English grad student Anoushka 'Noosh' Taylor is working as a junior reporter for a successful New York City radio network under the mentorship of her heroine, Allison Monroe. On the cusp of producing her first big story, an exposé of New York's BDSM club scene, Noosh is issued a challenge to go the extra mile and attend a club to see for herself. Summoning her courage, she finds herself caught up in a moment she can't escape with a devastatingly handsome man, and after being humiliated by him, she leaves in tears, vowing never to return.

Angry and hurt, Noosh drops the piece but cannot stop thinking about her almost lover.

When they decide to do a piece on the most eligible bachelor in

New York, Noosh is thrown into the path of Christofalo Montecito, playboy and son of organized crime boss, Fogliano Montecito. Christo is gorgeous, brooding, sensual – and the man who humiliated her at the BDSM club.

Noosh reacts badly, but when Christo apologizes, she begins to see a different side of him. Soon, their mutual attraction grows, and Noosh finds herself falling for Christo – but can a son of a crime boss ever be reliable, trustworthy?

When dark secrets from both of their pasts reveal themselves, Noosh and Christo have to decide whether their attraction is more than just a casual thing, and discover just how far they will go to save it.

Can Noosh give him the trust he has yet to earn? Or will Christo reveal himself to be his father's son?

CHAPTER ONE

Long Island, New York

CHRISTOFALO MONTECITO STARED at his father in astonishment. He *couldn't* be taking Christo's news this easily. *Nuh-uh, no way.* "Dad, you understand what I'm telling you?"

Fogliano Montecito gazed back at his son with the same brilliant green eyes he had bestowed on his only child. "Christo, do I look like an idiot? You want out of my business, that's the crux of the matter, right?"

Christo hesitated. "Right. Look, Dad, it's not as if I haven't mentioned this before, and I'm almost forty now, and it's time. I've given you the last seventeen years, all my time after college."

"College that my business paid for."

Here we go. "Yes, Dad, and I'm grateful for it, don't get me wrong. But I need to make my own way...and some aspects of the family business don't sit easily with me."

Fogliano held up his hands. "Enough. Christo, you must do

what you think is right, what is appropriate." He sighed and pushed back from his desk, standing and clapping his son on the back. "Now, you'll still be coming to the meal tonight?"

Christo, still stunned, nodded. "Sure, Dad."

"Good. Now, I have to get back to work. You can see yourself out?"

"Of course. See you later."

CHRISTO NODDED to his father's personal assistant, Mandy, who simpered at him. Christo tried not to roll his eyes and instead gave her a polite smile. At thirty-eight, with his father's Italian good looks and devastating smile, Christofalo Montecito had turned heads since he was a teenager. Wild dark curls, long, long legs and a body to die for meant that Christo had the pick of any women he wanted. And he took full advantage.

Lately, though, the constant stream of ready women was tiresome. *Where was the challenge, where was the fight?* Christo was feeling jaded by his entire lifestyle. Rich beyond imagination, he had begun to crave a simpler life, with a partner he could settle down with. Someone who would challenge him hold her own against the shattering weight of his family's reputation.

The Montecitos were well known in New York as one of the biggest family businesses – and that business was crime. Corruption, drugs, murder – Fogliano Montecito's reputation was feared by everyone, even his son. Christo had lost his mother to Fogliano's devotion to his corporation. Ornella Montecito had leaped to her death from the roof of the family's eighteen million dollar home in Sands Point, Long Island when Christo was seven years old, leaving her only son bewildered and broken. Christo had become an expert at shutting off his feelings after that, and after graduating *summa cum laude* from

Harvard Law, he had passively gone straight to work for his father.

Over the years, Christo had told himself that at least he, personally, was on the right side of the law, that he himself never oversaw anything that was *technically* illegal...but as he'd reached his late thirties, his conscience began to nag at him.

And there was something else. Christo, like his mother, had an artist's soul, and the more mired he got into practicing law, the more that side of him – and therefore his connection to his mother – faded. For the last couple of years he had been living a double life, and now that *other* life was the one he wanted to live. Hence the conversation with his father this morning.

Christo took the glass elevator from the top of his father's building down to the basement parking garage, and then slid into his Mercedes. He sighed, blowing out his cheeks, and dialed his best friend's number.

Bertie Franklin-Hart answered on the first ring. "Hey, dude, how'd it go?"

"It went...well." Christo knew Bertie would hear the astonishment in his voice, and by Bertie's silence, he knew Bertie was feeling it too.

"*Well?*" Total disbelief. Christo's mouth hitched up in a smile.

"Yup. Can you believe it?"

Bertie let out a long breath. "Well, no, to be honest. What's his game?"

Bertie, who had been Christo's roommate at Harvard, had no time for Christo's father or his associates, and was the only one of Christo's friends to say as much to his face. Bertie came from old money, older and even more powerful than the infamous Five Families and their successors. Bertie's money dated all the way back to the signing of the Declaration of Independence – and no one fucked with Bertie's family. *No one.*

Bertie sighed. "Well, I guess you're clear. Just, for me, take

Fogliano's word at face value for now, but don't trust him, Christo."

"I know. But it's the first step."

"I know you, Christo. You've got a glimpse of freedom, and you'll run at it full tilt. I love that about you, brother, but as your best friend...well...I got your back."

"Don't trust to hope." Christo's smile faded, although he knew Bertie was right. Fogliano wasn't someone people left behind without consequence, not even his own son.

"That's what I'm saying, but at the same time, go for it."

Christo mulled over his words. "Okay. Look, the dinner tonight?"

"I'll come, of course I'll come. I don't suppose there will be any chance of some beautiful women to distract us?"

Christo laughed. "No, it's one of Dad's sausage parties. But after...drinks at *La Forge*?"

"Deal."

NEW YORK CITY

ANOUSHKA 'NOOSH' Taylor shifted in her chair nervously as her boss, Allison, read through her proposal. Yes, it was her first big story, and yes, it was out there – even for a late-night radio talk show known for tackling dangerous subjects – but in her bones, Noosh knew Ally would go for it. It was the kind of story Allison Monroe had built her fearsome reputation on; a look into the BDSM clubs of New York's subculture. Noosh had spent months researching and talking to people who worked the clubs, and now she had put together a fifteen-minute segment for the show – her first chance to be on air.

Noosh had come to New York from London a year ago,

straight from a doctorate in creative writing, and now she had cultivated an honest and friendly working relationship with one of New York's major radio stars.

Allison Monroe was known for her exacting methods, razor-sharp intellect, and her ability to convey her natural warmth and vivacity with her interviewees. She set the proposal down now and looked at Noosh over her spectacles. Noosh's heart was pounding hard against her ribs; she couldn't read her boss's expression.

Allison studied her young friend for a minute then took her spectacles off, laying them gently down on her desk. "Noosh... how old are you again?"

Noosh felt her face redden. "Twenty-four."

"And I'm assuming you're not a virgin?"

The blush deepened. "No."

Allison sighed. "Sweetheart, while this proposal is well-written, obviously researched, and full of good intentions, it sounds like it was written by a virgin."

Noosh felt a lump settle on her chest. "Oh."

Allison smiled kindly at her. "I don't mean to be rude, darling, but here's my thing – there's a sense of 'Gosh, golly' about it. And by that, I mean you're painting this world as some kind of otherworldly experience that ordinary people don't subscribe to. The people you've interviewed here – hookers, security guards, club owners...what about the clientele? And I have one more major question which overrides all that."

"Which is?" Noosh tried to stop her voice from croaking with distress but failed, and Allison got up and came to sit on the desk in front of her.

"Noosh...did you actually *go* to the clubs?"

"Yes, of course," Noosh said defiantly. *Don't sulk, you're not a teenager.*

Allison smiled. "I mean, at night, as a client?"

Noosh was horrified. "No, of course not."

"See? How on earth can you expect to convince our listeners you're an expert on this subject if you yourself have no experience with the places? And Noosh, just so you know, BDSM is no longer a dirty little secret. With safety in mind, it can be a thrilling experience if that's where your particular peccadillos find their home." She sat back down behind her desk. "I'm not saying you have to go out and fuck a ton of men or get spanked by them, I'm just saying you should go, sit at the bar, have a drink and see what happens. Watch the interactions between people, talk to them. But don't tell them you're a journalist, for fuck's sake. Pretend you're the clientele for the night. You might surprise yourself."

Noosh's face was burning. "So..."

"So...keep working on it. There's promise, but it's not quite there yet." Allison handed the proposal back to Noosh. "Darling, it's coming along. I just think you need to go the extra mile. I'm pushing you because I believe in you. I believe you could be a rising star. I just want your debut to be as perfect as it should be."

NOOSH WAS STILL THINKING about Allison's words as she took the train home to her studio apartment in Queens. The 7 train was crowded and sweaty, and by the time she opened the door and dropped her bag on her floor, Noosh was exhausted. Coming from London, she was used to the hassle and annoyance of the Tube, so the actual train journey didn't bother her, just the amount of people. *Then why did you move to one of the most crowded cities in the world?*

To disappear...

Noosh pushed the thought away and stripped off her clothes. She thanked God she didn't have to wear a suit to work, that her usual uniform of blue jeans, t-shirt and Chuck Taylor's was accepted office attire. She didn't own anything that could be described as formal wear, except for the ruby-red dress she had worn for her graduation. She loved that dress. It had been a gift from her parents – her parents who had loved and supported her throughout her education, cheered her on, and scraped together their money to buy the designer dress for her. Noosh had worked and paid for her degrees with loans and grants – her parents would never have been able to afford to pay for it themselves.

Noosh had been born into a working-class family and had been brought up without wanting anything other than the food they provided and the love that they shared. In a modest two-up, two-down house out in the suburbs, both her parents worked as bank clerks and made sure that, even without the material things some of her classmates had, Noosh wanted for nothing.

To their credit, she had grown up with a strong work ethic, and their pride in their daughter knew no bounds as they watched her graduate with top honors from one of London's most prestigious universities.

Then it had all come crashing down. Noosh had been targeted by a powerful man who had set out to make her his – whether she wanted him or not. It had almost destroyed her. Now, she could hardly stand to think his name.

NOOSH STEPPED into the shower and turned on the hot water, enjoying the feel of the spray cleansing her tired skin. Her whole life now was work. Maybe Allison was right – maybe she should get out there, experience a little more of what this beautiful, vibrant city had to offer.

Supper was a bowl of cereal and then she fell asleep on the couch, not bothering to pull a blanket over herself. It was early fall in New York, still stifling hot on some days and Noosh wriggled uncomfortably in her sleep until she awoke at three a.m., sitting bolt upright. The thin drape at her window was billowing in. She'd left the window open. God, she never did that...*ever*. Not since...

Noosh skittered over to the window and slammed it shut, forgetting about the hour. She sent a silent apology to her neighbors upstairs. If only this studio weren't on the first floor, but the rent had been perfect for her budget and beggars couldn't be choosers. And baking in the heat of the non-air-conditioned apartment was a small price to pay for her safety.

After moving to her bed she found she couldn't sleep. She tried to read but by four had given up on that and was cleaning the apartment – again. She called it her 'Monica time' after the character from *Friends* – cleaning relaxed her, gave her time to think, to try and order her life a little better.

She thought back to what Allison had said. She *should* check out one of those clubs. The thought both scared and excited her. *Next week,* she told herself. *Next week, I'll go and see what gives in those places.* She blew out her cheeks. Yep, it would take a week to get her courage up, but she was determined to do it now. Finally, as the city began to wake, she fell asleep again and slept in until mid-morning.

SENATOR DESTRY PAPPS always woke at 5 a.m. sharp to begin his day. A six-mile run was followed by a shower then a breakfast of oatmeal and a protein shake, and then he was down in his office by 7.30 a.m. It had been his routine for at least a decade now, waking up in his Georgetown townhouse, a block from his office.

At fifty-three, Destry, a native of New York, had lived his entire life in politics. Following in his father's footsteps, he had become the senator for the District at thirty-eight and had remained in office for nearly two decades. He'd carefully planned his ascension through the party ranks and now he was, at last, going for the big job.

There was nothing Destry wanted more than to become President of the United States, and for the last couple of years he had been clearing house, ironing out anything that could stop him from realizing his goal. People were paid off, offered roles in his cabinet. His lovers, of which there had been many, had been vetted, and even his ex-wife, Telly, had been paid off to keep their dirty laundry private. Destry had no doubt that one day Telly would come to him with something more that she wanted from him, and it would be understood that whatever it was, Destry would provide it. But that was fine with him.

He checked his reflection out now. Tall, stately, with dark hair shot through with silver at the temples, he knew his handsome face was his ticket to getting what he wanted and had always used it. His patented 'aw-shucks' charm worked on the voting public as well as it did with his bed partners.

There was only one part of his life – as yet, a private part – that he reflected on with anger and resentment. The time in London, the time he'd seen *her* and felt his whole world shift. That dark, thick wavy hair, those large chocolate-brown eyes, that full mouth. Destry Papps had pursued Anoushka Taylor with the subtlety of a wrecking ball, and even his closest advisors had been scared by his passion for the girl. She was thirty years the Senator's junior, a grad student, and an unknown quantity.

What Destry knew and no one else did was that Anoushka – his Noosh – had resisted his charms at first, had expressed doubts over their relationship. At least, she did until he wore her down, first by love-bombing her, promising her that he would give it all up for her, and then when she showed signs of independence from him, he'd shown her in an entirely different way that had nothing to do with love.

She'd escaped him, finally, disappearing from London entirely. He'd tracked her down, though, to a cottage in the north of England. Destry had made sure Noosh knew how angry he was.

He thought of her now, how she'd cringed away from his rage, and he smiled. He could still feel her skin under his fingertips, her mouth on his as he took her. He'd told her then, "If you ever leave me again, I'll kill you." And he had meant it.

Then Noosh did the unthinkable and tried to commit suicide. Her parents, those seemingly weak fools, had spirited her away from the hospital in the middle of the night, and Noosh had disappeared – for real, this time. But she was there, out in the world somewhere and ready to use his behavior against him at the most critical moment. That couldn't be happen, obviously.

Which is why he had sent his best men out to scour the globe for her. There had been sightings – in London, in Mumbai, where her mother hailed from, in Sydney. Destry's gut instinct told him that she was somewhere in plain sight, but it frustrated him that she was so well hidden.

"Come out, come out, wherever you are." Destry closed the door to his office and flicked on his computer. He ignored the hundreds of emails and instead clicked on his private folder. Photo after photo of her, always with that haunted look in her eyes. Broken. Beautiful. He traced the outline of her face and sighed. "I can't let you live, my darling. Not without me. Never without me." He closed his eyes, imagining his hands around her throat, squeezing, or driving a knife deep into her gut as she begged for her life. His dick hardened, and he wondered if he could risk jerking off before his assistant got into the office. He heard someone moving in the outer office and sighed, closing the folder. "Another time, my love."

He picked up the phone and called his Head of Security. "Any news?"

"No, Destry. We haven't found anything on where she might be,"

"Jesus...she's just one woman, for fuck's sake. How hard can it be?"

His employee apologized. "I promise we'll find her, it just may take some time."

"I'm announcing my candidacy in two weeks. I don't want anything spoiling that moment. Find her. That's all I ask of you. When you do, I'll take care of her."

"Boss, if I find her, I'll end her. There's no need for you..."

"No," Destry said, interrupting him. "I'll be the one to kill Anoushka. *Me.* Just tell me where to find her."

He hung up the phone and smiled to himself. He could hardly wait.

CHAPTER TWO

Christo pushed his food around his plate, not hungry. He was all too aware of the brooding figure of his father at the end of the dining table. His father's business associates, some of Christo's uncles and cousins, and Bertie too, were all there as well, but Christo could feel his father's scrutiny. He met his father's gaze with a question in his eyes. Fogliano had been quiet all throughout the meal, but now he tapped his fork on his glass, asking for their attention.

"Friends, family, thank you for coming this evening, on what, to my surprise, is quite an auspicious night."

Christo's back stiffened, and Bertie shot him a warning look. *Let your father say his piece.* Christo sighed. He had no idea what his father would tell the others and so had no defense prepared.

Fogliano smiled, but there was no warmth in it. "My son, my only child, came to me today and told me he didn't want my business."

"And here we go," breathed Bertie under his breath. Christo's gaze never left his father's.

"Now," Fogliano continued, "I have always been proud of my son, proud of what he has achieved, of how much he has given me, and so the fact he wants to make his own way in the world is pleasing to me."

Christo's eyes widened slightly, and he relaxed a little. Fogliano smiled a little. "And do you know what my son, my Harvard-educated lawyer son, wants to do with his life now that he no longer wishes to be part of our working life?"

Christo's hope faded. Nope, this wasn't going to be a rousing speech singing his praises. He knew the look in his father's eyes – he was about to be roasted, broiled alive, mocked mercilessly. *Well, bring it, Pa. I can handle it.*

"He wants to make *furniture!*" Fogliano spat triumphantly. "Furniture! Like some damn hipster fool in the Village, can you believe it? I'm so glad I spent hundreds of thousands of dollars on your education, son, so that you can prance around with your bespoke hand-crafted side tables and rocking chairs. Such a privilege to be able to say that my son, who I raised as my heir to the business I have given my life to create...wants *nothing* to do with it. How is it I have raised such an ungrateful child?"

The room was silent, the atmosphere thick and unsettling as Fogliano got up and moved down the table to his son. Christo gritted his teeth. This was going to be one of Fogliano's rants, clearly. *I should have known,* Christo thought, *I should have known he wouldn't take it well, that he was waiting to humiliate me in front of everyone.* He caught Bertie's eyes. Bertie's expression was angry but watchful. Christo shook his head – he knew Bertie would stand up to his father in defense of his friend, but Christo felt numb. *So be it,* he thought, *bring it on, Dad. Do your worst.*

The anger that had been building inside him for years now was almost at its peak. As Fogliano bore down on his son, Christo got to his feet. "What's up, Dad? Can't bear the thought of someone making an honest buck for a change?"

Fogliano stopped. "An *honest* buck? I've had just about enough of your moralizing, boy. My money was good enough to feed you, clothe you, put you through college and now you're too good for it?"

Christo squared up to his father. "No, Pa. I'm not good. I'll never be good, but I can try to redress the balance. For Mom, as well as myself."

He knew mentioning Ornella would set his father off, but Christo didn't care. He wanted to push Fogliano, wanted that fight to happen so he could feel good about making the break. He didn't have to wait long. Fogliano cold-cocked him, and he slammed into the table, crashing against the plates and cutlery. The men around the table shot to their feet as Fogliano hauled his son up and hit him again. Bertie lunged forward, but Christo shouted for him to stop. Fogliano beat his son again until Christo's nose poured with blood. The room was silent as Fogliano let Christo go, his own breath ragged.

"Get out of my house," he growled, his face a mask of pure rage. Christo got unsteadily to his feet and looked his father in the eyes.

"My fucking *pleasure*."

He let Bertie steer him out of the mansion and into Bertie's car. Christo gazed up at the house as Bertie drove him away from it, knowing he would never see it again. He was free.

"Dude, let's get to the club," he said, wiping the blood from his face. "I need a drink...or seven."

It wasn't until, very drunk, he went home to his apartment that night, that Christo let himself break.

Two weeks later and Noosh still hadn't summoned the courage to go to the sex club. She had quietly pushed her story aside and helped out with Allison's punishing schedule, hoping her boss would simply forget about it, but then, one Thursday night as they shared pizza late in the evening, Allison studied her. "So?"

Noosh feigned ignorance. "So, what?"

Allison rolled her eyes. "Noosh."

Noosh sighed. "So...it's on hold."

"Until?"

"Until I can persuade myself to go to the club. I mean, you're right. I need to experience it, it's just...I'm not sure BDSM is my thing."

"Do you suppose journalists who go to war-torn countries like what they have to see? The story's the thing, not your personal preferences. Besides, I never said you had to try out any of that stuff." Allison shoved a piece of pizza into her mouth and studied Noosh. "When was the last time you got laid, anyway?"

Noosh laughed, half-shocked, although it was exactly the kind of thing Allison would come out with. "A while," Noosh answered honestly, then grinned at her boss. "And you?"

"Last night. A delectable lawyer from mid-town. Nice guy. Big cock."

Noosh almost spat her soda out, laughing. She shook her head at her boss. "You're incorrigible."

"And satisfied. God, Noosh, have you looked in the mirror? You could have any man you wanted, you know that, right?"

Noosh felt the cold hand close over her heart – the way it had ever since *him*. "I don't want a man. I'm fine the way I am."

Allison harrumphed, unconvinced, but was distracted by her phone beeping. "Oh, here we go. Senator Papps has announced. Thought that might be coming."

Noosh wondered if her shock was visible on her face. "Destry Papps?"

"Yup. Mr. Smooth is running for President, and the way I hear it, he has a pretty good shot."

Noosh felt sick but covered her distress by tidying up their dinner things. "That's not something we'll cover though, right? I mean, politics isn't really in our remit."

Allison brushed crumbs off her pants. "Not directly, but Papps is popular with women. Good-looking guy."

Noosh felt her face burn. "Not my type."

Allison, missing Noosh's red face, chuckled. "Well, he's a bit too polished for my taste too, but each to their own. Hey, are you okay?"

Finally, she had noticed that Noosh was looking sick. Noosh nodded. "Just tired."

"Well, let's get you a cab – god, it's way past eleven, Noosh, why didn't you say? You must think me a real taskmaster." She smiled at her young friend. "Sweetheart, take tomorrow off, and Monday. Have a long weekend, and get some rest. Don't think I haven't noticed how much work you put in here – it is very much appreciated. I don't often say this, but these last few months you really have made me excited about this job again."

As she sat in the backseat of her cab on the way to her apartment, Noosh concentrated on Allison's compliments. It felt so good to hear her heroine, her idol, her mentor say those things to her, but still, the evening had been tarnished by the thought of Destry.

God...

Noosh felt like throwing up, imagining him as President. Of course, if anyone could stop that, it would be her. She could tell a thousand stories of his hateful, vicious personality. His violence...his threats to kill her.

But even if anyone actually believed her, going to the press or the police would be as good as signing her own death warrant.

As she trudged into her apartment, making sure the deadbolt was on, she realized a hard truth. If Destry ever found her... she had no doubt she would be dead. Why the hell had she come to America? To *his* home? Was it spite? Was it to hide in plain sight?

No. *Fuck him.* It was to pursue her dream of being a radio journalist – to work with Allison – to have something for herself. She had already lost so much because of him... Seeing her parents, for one. She missed them so much and lived for the phone calls to the burner phones she replaced every week. Her friends back in London, her extended family in Mumbai. All of them were out of bounds now, because of the chance Destry might use them to find her. Even at work she used a pseudonym for her writing credits – Sarah Marsh. Something completely unconnected with her real name.

Noosh lay on her bed, staring sleeplessly at the ceiling. To live under a death threat was still unreal and yet all too real to her. It made her angry, and full of sorrow.

She rolled onto her side. *You know what? I will go the club, and maybe I will fuck some random guy there...because I can Destry. It'll be my choice. Screw you and your political ambitions. If I hear one – just one story – of you treating another woman like me, I'll go public, and hang the consequences.*

I will bring your house of cards down, even if it costs me my own life.

CHAPTER THREE

Bertie glanced over at his friend. Christo was drinking steadily now, his handsome face set in anger. He had been like this ever since that terrible night at his father's house, and Bertie was worried. Christo had never been a big drinker, and to see him throw back expensive whiskey as if it were soda was wrong somehow. Between the two of them, Christo was usually the down-to-earth one, the one who would prop up Bertie after a night out, the one who would stop drinking before the hangover set in.

Now, though, his friend was on a knife's edge, and Bertie didn't know how the hell to pull him back from it. He sat up as Christo lurched from the bar stool and staggered towards the door. "Dude, where the hell are you going?"

"To get laid." Christo shot back darkly, and Bertie sighed. That was the other thing. Endless women – a different one every night for the last few weeks. Christo waking up in a stranger's house every time, from which Bertie had to pick him up.

"Christo, I'm flying to LA in the morning. I won't be there to pick you up."

Christo stopped at the door, turning to gave his friend a sad smile. "You've been picking me up too many times, my friend. It's time you let me fall where I need to, even if it's the gutter."

Bertie was surprised at how lucid, if depressed, his friend sounded. He got up and went to him. "Come on, Christo, let me take you home instead. Get some rest."

Christo considered but then shook his head. "It's okay, Bertie. I'll go to my club...they know how to put me in a cab. I need to fuck, Bertie. I need to get this rage out somehow, and fucking is the least destructive way I can think of."

Bertie sighed. "The women are okay with that?"

"They just want to fuck too." Christo, his green eyes sad, looked away from his friend's scrutiny. "Let me go, Bert. I need to do this my way. I'll come out of it, I promise."

Bertie watched helplessly as Christo walked out of the bar and hailed a cab. Christo was right – the only person who could pull him out of this slump was himself. Bertie almost couldn't believe this was the result of Christo finally freeing himself from his father. He was so sure that his friend would be celebratory, not depressed. He'd gotten what he wanted, right? So why was he so self-destructive? Had his father's beating really fucked with his head that much?

Bertie shook his head and went back to collect his jacket. One thing he knew for sure was this: Christo was right – Bertie had to let him fall before he could begin to help him get back on his feet.

He just hoped it wouldn't be too late.

NOOSH WAS DEBATING whether to walk into the club confidently, or to simply just throw up. She shivered in the night air despite it being very warm, and then smoothed her dress down for the fourteenth time. "Option one," she told herself, and lifted her chin, stepping into the club's entrance. The security man at the door nodded politely to her and opened the door. Noosh thanked him, making sure her voice didn't shake before walking in.

A wash of music came over her, and as she walked into the bar area, a thousand different thoughts invaded her mind. Her vision was bombarded by the sights to her left, where a small stage showed people writhing and dancing, all naked and sweaty.

Okay, she told herself, *you expected this. Don't freak out. Don't look like a rookie.*

She walked steadily to the bar and sat down. The bartender greeted her – everyone was so polite – and she ordered a cosmopolitan. Sipping her drink, she took her time to look around.

At a table in the corner, a woman dressed entirely in latex was blindfolding a man, who was stripped down to his jeans. When he couldn't see, the woman picked up a candle and dripped hot wax onto his chest – slowly – smiling as he groaned. Other people watched them, but the connection between the two of them was so palpable that Noosh couldn't look away. The dominatrix caught her eye and smiled. Noosh smiled back.

The atmosphere of the club surprised her. Unlike the sweaty, handsy feel of the usual Friday night clubs, here was a relaxed, open atmosphere that astonished her. After an hour, she was even enjoying watching what was going, which seemed to be okay by everyone, even if she didn't join in.

Noosh had to admit that the overtly open atmosphere was erotic, and when a beautiful woman came up to order a drink at the bar and turned to her, surprising her with a soft kiss on the mouth, Noosh went with it.

"You're beautiful," the woman said, stroking her hands up Noosh's thighs, "but overdressed. First time?"

Noosh nodded shyly. The woman, a gorgeous, voluptuous

blonde, nodded her head towards the opposite side of the bar, grinning. "There's a man who has been gazing at you and you alone for an hour. He's sensational. Go, enjoy."

Noosh looked over to where the blonde nodded, and her stomach gave a strange lurch of pure desire. 'Sensational' didn't begin to cover it.

The man met her gaze. His eyes were bright green, contrasting to great effect with his dark hair and beard, and they burned into Noosh's. Her body reacted to him immediately; her nipples hardened almost painfully, and her cunt flooded with arousal.

She couldn't catch her breath. The man slid from his seat and walked towards her, and Noosh couldn't move. He was tall, at least a foot taller than her five-five, and as he reached her, he stared down at her, not speaking. For a moment they just gazed at each other, then he bent his head, and his mouth met hers.

The kiss was soft at first, but as Noosh gave into it, his lips became hungry against hers. Finally, breaking away only because she ran out of oxygen, Noosh felt her entire body tremble uncontrollably. Who *was* this man?

She opened her mouth to speak, but he shook his head, taking her hand and leading her deeper into the club. Noosh went with him because not doing so was unthinkable. They walked for what seemed like miles, until they reached a locked door. Her companion unlocked it and drew her inside. He didn't pause as he locked the door before sliding his hands around her waist, kissing her again, pressing his body against hers.

Noosh tangled her hands in his hair, pulling on the dark curls as she kissed him back, her mind swirling with delirious pleasure. She could feel the hot length of his cock through his pants, pressing against her belly. She moaned slightly at the thought of what they were about to do.

Her moan seemed to set something off in him, and he

tugged down the straps of her dress, exposing her breasts to his mouth. His lips fixed themselves on her nipple, making her gasp. She could feel an orgasm already beginning to build, but she wanted to prolong this pleasure as long as she could.

Tentatively, she snaked her hand down to his fly, unzipping his pants and sliding her hand in, feeling his cock harden against her hand. God, he was *huge*...

He was pushing up her skirt then tearing at her underwear, and Noosh felt a desperate need to have him inside her. Her lover rolled a condom quickly down the length of his ram-rod hard cock and then, with a confident thrust, he entered her.

Noosh gave a shaky gasp as they began to fuck, clawing at each other, kissing as if they wanted to devour each other. He pressed her up against the wall and took her, his arms easily holding her up, his cock driving deeper and deeper into her with every stroke. His eyes never left hers.

Noosh moaned as he thrust harder, deeper, and for the first time she saw in his eyes anger, rage, and something else...pain. She kissed him fiercely, wanting to take that pain – whatever it was – away.

But then her eyes were rolling back in her head, and she cried out as her orgasm hit her hard. His free hand was stroking her clit, his mouth on hers...he knew exactly what he was doing.

With a groan he came too, and they tumbled to the floor. Noosh caught her breath, enjoying the feel of his weight on her. After a moment he sat up, breathing hard. Noosh pulled her dress up and sat by him.

After a long moment, when she thought he would never say anything, he turned to her. God, he was so beautiful... As he opened his mouth to speak, Noosh couldn't help but touch his face. It seemed to take him by surprise. She cupped his cheek in her hand, stroking her thumb gently over his skin, taking in every detail of his face. If she never saw him again, she wanted to remember everything.

The atmosphere changed between them then. No longer did he look like a glowering, dangerously sexual man, but someone vulnerable, tired...sad. He closed his eyes as she stroked his face, leaning into her touch.

Then he pulled away, pain creasing his handsome face. "Don't."

Stung, Noosh withdrew her hand. "I'm sorry, it's just..."

"We're here to fuck. Fucking is all I do now."

His voice was hard, and he no longer looked at her.

"Did I do something wrong?"

"*Jesus.*" He hissed out the word. "Look, I'm not into schooling newbies. I come here to fuck and be fucked, not to deal with some virgin."

He got up and Noosh scrambled to her feet, her heart pounding. How had things turned so quickly? "I'm no virgin," she managed to say, her voice only slightly shaking.

She glanced around the room and saw a cabinet of paddles, ropes, leather crops, and other toys. She swallowed hard and looked back at him. He was watching her again, glowering from beneath his long, thick lashes. She lifted her chin and deliberately dropped the shoulder straps of her dress, exposing her breasts. "Fuck me again and I'll show you just how far from a virgin I really am."

"No."

God, that hurt. She wouldn't beg this man, this glorious man, whose pain she could see etched across his gorgeous face. But she didn't want the memory of their coupling sullied by this... whatever *this* was. What had she done wrong? She pulled the straps of her dress up, taking a deep breath in. She stepped towards him, saw he didn't back away. "What is it?" She asked him gently. "Why are you in so much pain?"

"I think you should go. You don't belong here."

"Neither do you."

He gave a short, humorless laugh. "Sweetheart, you have no idea what you're talking about. Please, just go."

With her thighs still aching from the fucking her gave her, Noosh stood her ground. *No.* She would not walk away. There had been something here, something worth exploring. She knew he felt it too.

Her lover shook his head. "Get out. Please, just go, I can't bear this."

Her heart gave a sickening lurch. "No. I won't go."

"Please."

She stepped forward and reached out to him, but he backed away, his hands curling into tight fists by his side. "Get out...now. While you still can."

A thrill of danger went through her. "No."

A silence, then he stalked across the room and dragged her to the door. Noosh laid her hands on his chest as she put her back against the door. "No, you don't get to throw me away like that. Not after that... That was incredible..."

He closed his eyes. "Please, I'm begging you. Go. *Go.*"

"But..."

"*Go!*"

The ferocity of the roar coming from this man, this dangerous man who towered above her, finally broke her resolve. Noosh fumbled for the door handle and opened the door, skittering down the hallway, hearing him slam the door behind her. She raced through the club, not bothering to look at anything else as she took the stairs to the doorway.

It was only when she stepped – barefoot – out onto the streets of New York City that she realized she was crying.

· · ·

THE MAN SAT in the car parked opposite the club and smiled to himself. He wondered if he should go over, say hello, help her get home…but that wasn't why he was here. He had been tasked with finding Anoushka Taylor, and after a tip, he had finally found where she lived. He had to confirm the address was right before he contacted the boss, however, and after seeing her at the club, he'd followed her here. Who knew the girl was into kink? It made his dick hard to think of her like that, but now, seeing her in tears, he realized she must be new to the scene.

He snickered to himself and pulled out his cell phone. Destry Papps answered on the first ring.

The man in the car watched Anoushka Taylor hail a cab and smiled into the phone. "Yeah, it's me. I found her."

CHAPTER FOUR

After she'd gone, Christo slumped to the floor, breathing deeply. God, what had he become? Screaming at that girl, that sweet, kind, beautiful girl? And yet, it was her sweetness that had made him react like that. He didn't deserve her. The way she had touched his face, the way she had *seen* him...

"Fuck. *Fuck.*" He cursed quietly, his head in his hands. *Go after her, apologize, beg her to come back*. But he knew he couldn't. The moment he saw her earlier, something had twisted inside him. She was so lovely, her big brown eyes warm and kind, and she looked so lost. He'd wanted to take her in his arms, protect her from the seediness around them, but as soon as he kissed her, something animal had taken over. Making love to her was exhilarating – her voluptuous body curving against his, his cock driving deep into her velvety cunt...it had been an awakening to him. He'd never felt that way with any woman...and it terrified him.

He tried to stop the sobs that were constricting his chest, but they burst out anyway. What the fuck was happening to him?

Bertie was right; he'd gotten what he wanted – away from his father. So why was he so goddamn miserable?

He let himself cry it out then snagged his phone from his pocket and dialed Bertie. When his friend answered, he just said "Rock bottom."

Bertie understood immediately. "Where are you?"

Christo told him, and Bertie told him to stay there. "I'm coming to get you."

In an hour, Christo was on a plane to Arizona where Bertie booked him into rehab.

NOOSH BURIED herself in her work after that strange, wonderful, terrible night. She'd told Allison she was dropping the story about the BDSM clubs, and although Allison had questioned her about what had happened, Noosh kept it to herself. She felt wrecked by the experience, but at the same time, she couldn't stop thinking about her mercurial lover. Who was he? In moments of weakness, she closed her eyes and remembered the feel of his hands on her body, his mouth against hers, his cock thrusting deep inside her. She shivered, the pleasure all still too real for her. But then afterward...

Stop thinking about him, she told herself now. *It's been a month. You'll never see him again.* She dragged her attention back to the meeting. They were brainstorming ideas for the next year's stories and so far, Noosh hadn't heard a thing.

She blinked and focused on what Allison was saying. "Something I was thinking about was the next generation of New York's crime families. A lot of them are eschewing the old life and branching out on their own with legitimate businesses. I've heard the reaction from the old timers has been...mixed, to say the least. I'd like to focus in on three or four of the heirs who have broken free."

"Any ideas on who and how?" Seth, one of the station's head honchos, looked interested.

Allison nodded, her grey eyes serious. "A four-part series. I interview each of them, ask them the hard questions about how they feel about their family mob connections and why they chose to break free. Hang on, I have a list here." She dug around in her notebook. "Richard Viera, Dominick Octavo, Christofalo Montecito, and Helena De Vito. Those are the names I came up with through very basic research."

Seth nodded, and Noosh wrote down the names, glad of something else to concentrate on. "I like your thinking, Ally," Seth said and nodded at Noosh. "You'll work together with Allison on this?"

Noosh smiled gratefully. "Love to."

Allison winked at her. "And then, we can't ignore that it's election year next year. With any luck, we'll get the candidates in for an interview."

"Will they want to be associated with such a cutting-edge show as yours?" Felix, a snide show runner who loathed Allison and her talent, interjected, but Seth waved his hand.

"We'll get the ones who have enough guts, the ones who willingly go on Colbert. They're the ones we want. Harper, Seagram, Papps – they're the ones we want – or don't want, in the case of some of them."

"Destry Papps would be a get." Allison conceded, and Noosh's heart sank. *God, no.* She knew instantly she'd be calling in sick the day Destry came into the station. She found that her fingernails were digging into her palm, leaving deep welts, and flexed her fingers.

After the meeting, she hunkered back down in her cubicle and worked her way through the paperwork, immersing herself in admin work. It was only when Allison came by her desk that she looked at the clock and realized it was past eight p.m.

"Hey, kiddo, time you went home. But before you do, I've been thinking. You know, this mob-heir thing – this could be the thing you take the lead on, and I'll tell you why it could be interesting. You're not from New York or even the States. Your perspective as an outsider could be the thing that makes them open up to you. What do you say?"

Noosh gaped at her boss. To be asked to lead such a huge story was incredible. "I don't know what to say."

"Say yes," Allison grinned, then her smile faded. "Noosh, you deserve this, and there's something else... I don't know what happened to you at that club, but I know something did, and I feel bad. I encouraged you to go, and whatever happened – "

"Whatever happened, happened," Noosh interrupted her. "It's not your fault."

There was a long silence. "Who was he?"

Noosh struggled for a moment to find the words, and decided the truth was the only way to go. "The most incredible man I've ever met. And the most damaged. Not a good combination."

Allison patted her shoulder. "I'm sorry, honey. I've known men like that. They're instantly addictive, like sugar or heroin, but so, so bad for you."

Noosh nodded but looked away from her boss's gaze. "I agree."

"Anyway, sweetheart, go home and we'll talk more about this in the morning. The mob stories, I mean, although you know you can talk to me about anything."

Noosh smiled at her. "I know. Thanks, I'll see you tomorrow."

On the subway home, Noosh indulged in another fantasy about her mysterious lover, imagining him turning up at her apartment door, begging for her forgiveness. Would she make him beg? Noosh smirked to herself. Probably not – one look at those green eyes of his and she would cave. *Pathetic,* she told herself, but still visualized pulling him into her apartment, tearing off his clothes and fucking him until they were both exhausted.

At home, she took a long soak in the bathtub, indulging the fantasy some more, her hand between her legs, caressing her clit, imagining it was his tongue on her. She shivered through a mellow orgasm before pushing thoughts of him away.

Maybe some people were just meant to be experienced once in a lifetime, she told herself, as she pulled the comforter over her shoulders and settled down to watch the television.

NOOSH NEVER KNEW what woke her. Whether it was the sound of the television, which was still on, or the sense of someone being in the room with her. Noosh opened her eyes and froze. A dark figure was standing next to her sofa bed. She barely had time to try and make out his or her features before whoever it was shot her, the flash of the muzzle lighting up the room as he pumped three bullets into Noosh's belly, the sound muffled by a silencer.

Noosh gasped, stunned. The pain hit her full force she knew one thing for sure as she lay bleeding out.

Destry had found her.

CHAPTER FIVE

Six months later...

THE PHYSIOTHERAPIST GAVE her a long stare. "Noosh, you're pushing yourself too hard. I told you this would take time."

Noosh, balancing herself between the bars, shook her head. "Doc, it's been *too* long. I'm going stir-crazy in this hospital. I want to go back to work."

The doctor, a tired-looking woman in her thirties named Beth, rolled her eyes. "And don't think I don't know you've been working from your room. Rest is anathema to you, isn't it?"

"I had plenty of rest when I was brought in." Noosh propelled herself painfully along the treadmill. One good thing about having a bullet in the spine, it sure helped your upper body strength when you tried to learn to walk again, she thought, as she puffed her way along the walkway.

"For the record, a coma isn't rest, Noosh. Come on, that's it for today." Beth helped Noosh back into her chair. Noosh gave a frustrated sigh.

"Come on, Beth, do a girl a solid and let me out of here."

Beth couldn't help but grin. "Just so you know, that expression coming from your English mouth sounds weird. And, okay then."

Noosh was already geared up for an argument, so Beth's agreement took her by surprise. "Really?"

"Really." Beth nevertheless insisted on wheeling Noosh back to her room. "Tomorrow, and I mean it. Get some sleep tonight, and if your stats are good in the morning, you can go home. I'm not happy about you being alone, though."

"I won't be alone, for the most part."

Noosh's parents had been flown over by the radio station after Noosh had been shot, but when it had been clear their daughter would survive, they'd had to return to their lives in London, albeit Skyping Noosh every day. Allison, shaken to her core by the attempted murder, had sworn to them that she would take care of Noosh, and had insisted Noosh move in with her in her Upper East Side apartment.

"With *security*," she'd emphasized when Noosh protested, and Noosh couldn't argue. The man – she presumed it was a man – who had shot her was still out there, and the police had no leads. Noosh hadn't told them of her suspicions – that Senator Destry Papps, candidate for the office of the President of the United States, was the one who had shot her mercilessly. Who the hell would believe that? Her mother and father had looked at her with pain in their eyes, and she knew they guessed the same. Would Destry try again?

Noosh hoped against hope that by not revealing him now, he would understand she wouldn't go the press about him at all, but she knew that was a naïve hope. So the promise of being secure, at least at home, was appealing.

Allison had been to see her every day, and Noosh knew from the topics of conversation on her radio show that the shooting had affected her usually unflappable boss to the core. Allison had persuaded the station to run an anti-firearms campaign, and by sharing Noosh's – or rather, 'Sarah's' – story with her listeners, Allison had managed to both bring awareness to the subject and, Noosh hoped, to broadcast to the assailant that she was now going to be protected.

Noosh knew Destry had heard the program because the day after, a huge bouquet of red roses had arrived for her with the card just saying "*Sarah...*" on it. Funny how threatening just that one word could be, she mused as she'd dumped the flowers into the trash can.

ALLISON INSISTED on coming personally to pick her up from the hospital after Noosh was discharged, and she settled Noosh into the back seat of the limousine, fussing around her, making Noosh grin. "You really have gone full-on Momma-Bear, haven't you?"

"Quiet, child," Allison said, hiding her grin. "Now, your mom and dad packed all your things and sent them to me, so I took the liberty of unpacking some non-personal stuff, just to make your room feel like home."

Noosh sighed. It had taken her months to find the apartment in Queens, and having to let it go was annoying. *But you're alive, so stop feeling sorry for yourself and buck up.* Noosh smiled her thanks at Allison and changed the subject.

"How are the interviews going?" Noosh had missed the preparation and setting up of the Mobster Heirs series, and was sorry to have been out of action for it. From what Allison told her, it had been an eye-opening experience.

"Good so far, but we have one hold-out...at least, we did.

Christofalo Montecito called the day after our firearms campaign - and your story - got coverage on the national news. Said he wanted to help out with that, and if he could, he would give us the interview we want."

"That's good news. What's his story?"

"Hard to say. We know he's broken away from his family's business, but what he's been doing, what he plans to do, is a mystery. Try researching someone who doesn't want to be found. There are no photos, no gossip about the man at all. Unheard of these days, but the man's a ghost."

Noosh was surprised. "That is unheard of."

Allison grinned at her. "I know what you're thinking – that you can find something on the internet even if an old coot like me can't, but...there's nothing. The man's a private guy. So, him coming in to see us..."

Noosh groaned. "Tell me I can be there! I've missed out on *everything*, Ally."

Allison sighed. "Alright, you can be there, but – and I mean this – you are not to do *anything* but watch and say hello to the man."

Noosh grumbled but agreed. "When is he coming in?"

"Thursday...and as part of the deal, until then, you rest."

"Fine."

"Grumpuss."

"Shut up."

CHRISTO WALKED out of his bathroom to find Bartie waiting in his kitchen, helping himself to Christo's coffee. He smiled at his friend. "How do I look?"

Bertie looked him up and down, snickering. "Ugly as sin, but smart enough."

"Thanks, dude." Christo laughed. He knew he looked good

in the navy sweater and dark jeans, but he was nervous as hell. Bertie studied him.

"Dude, relax. This will be a breeze. All you have to do is talk about your new business."

Christo rolled his eyes. "We both know that's not true."

Bertie grinned, unrepentant. "You got me. Look, just stick to the truth – it's easier to remember. Mr. Montecito, did you ever knowingly participate in illegal activities?"

"No."

"But you knew your father's business was linked to organized crime?"

Christo sighed. "Yes."

"Don't sigh. Just say yes. Look, buddy, of course they're going to ask you the hard questions. You knew this and agreed to the interview anyway."

Christo nodded. "I listened to the other interviews." He began to smile. "Helena really met her match, huh?"

Bertie clutched his heart dramatically. "Do not speak ill of the lovely Helena."

Christo laughed. "Bert, you know what would actually make your fantasy real? Asking Helena out. Come on."

He grabbed his keys and Bertie followed him out of the apartment. "That," Bertie said sniffily, "would involve me speaking to her, which I am not."

"Because she beat you at squash?"

Bertie grumbled under his breath and Christo snickered. "Dude, let it go. Trust me, Helena is a pussy cat."

"God, you've fucked her, haven't you?" As they got into Christo's car, Bertie sounded half-angry, half-admiring. Christo shook his head.

"No, I promise you I haven't. Not Helena, not knowing how you feel about her. I'm glad I didn't sink that low."

Bertie clapped his friend's shoulder. "Good boy." Bertie sat back as Christo pulled the car out into traffic. Christo had always insisted on driving himself, even when he worked for his father, and Bertie watched the streets flow by. After a while, he turned to his friend.

"So..."

"Yeah?"

"You still obsessing over the club girl?"

Christo shot him a look. "I don't want to talk about her."

"But you're still hung up?"

Christo sighed, then nodded. "I can't get her out of my head, Bert. She was so lovely, and I treated her like crap. I would be damn lucky to find a girl like that, and I blew it. All I think about is finding her and apologizing."

"One of your twelve steps?"

Christo grinned despite himself. "You're such a douche bag."

"True dat."

They drove in companionable silence for a while, then Bertie cleared his throat. "How about putting a private detective on the case? See if he can find her?"

Christo rolled his eyes. "Yes, dude, because invading her privacy just so I can feel better *is* the way to go."

"Fair point. Thought about going back to the club?"

Christo shook his head. "No. Look, can we change the subject?"

"Of course, brother."

Ten minutes later they were pulling into the parking lot of the radio station, and Christo hesitated. Bertie waited until Christo nodded. "Let's do this."

They were greeted by a bubbly blonde intern, Liam, who was flirtatious and fun and made them relax a little. "Now, once you have your studio i.d., take the elevator to the third floor and follow the hallway around to Studio C. Noosh will look after you from there. You can't miss her – gorgeous, sexy, and going hell for leather in a wheelchair at the moment."

Christo and Bertie rode the elevator, and Christo blew out his cheeks. Bertie grinned at him. "Not too late to back out."

Christo shook his head. "I'm good."

They followed the hallway as directed and finally came to the door of Studio C. Christo, his mouth dry, stopped at the water cooler outside of the studio as Bertie knocked on the door, opening it to speak to the woman inside.

"Hey, are you Noosh? Hi, I'm Bertie, Mr. Montecito's assistant."

Christo heard a soft voice. "Oh, hey, nice to meet you, I'm Noosh Taylor. Come on in, Ally's just setting up. I'll tell her you're here."

"Oh, hey, do you need a hand?"

"No, it's okay, I'm just getting used to this thing. I don't really need it, but Ally insists. Won't be a moment."

There was something familiar about the voice, and Christo stepped into the room just as the woman turned away from him. *No. No way.* His heart began to beat faster as he recognized the soft wavy hair falling down her back, the caramel skin, the curvy body, now sitting in a wheelchair. *How? Why?*

He made an involuntary noise, and she looked up. Her face paled as she stared back at him with a mixture of horror and shock.

It was her. It was his sweet girl.

CHAPTER SIX

Noosh stared at him, her heart pounding painfully against her ribs. After a moment, she remembered where she was and cleared her throat. Unsmiling, she nodded to him and turned back to Bertie. "Ally will be out in a second. Can I get either of you some coffee?"

"Please, don't trouble yourself," Christo Montecito said in that deep, sensual voice of his, and Noosh felt her belly quiver with desire. *No. Nope, this wasn't happening.* She looked away from that intense green-eyed stare, the curiosity in them. She knew he was wondering about her wheelchair and felt a wash of embarrassment. She leveraged herself out of the chair, wobbling, and both Bertie and Christo stepped forward to help her. She waved them away, her face burning. "I'm fine."

Ally opened the door at that particular moment – *damn it* – and made a frustrated noise. "Again, Noosh? What was our deal?"

Noosh's face flamed even redder. "I was just practicing. Anyway, our guests are here."

Ally immediately switched into her professional mode. "Bertie, how nice to see you again."

Bertie winked at her. "You too, Ally, looking good. Can I introduce my friend, Christofalo Montecito?"

Ally shook Christo's hand and Noosh could see her boss sizing him up. She risked another glance at the man. If it were possible, he was even more beautiful than she remembered, and he looked better, healthier than when she'd met him in the club. His olive skin was smooth, his beard neatly trimmed, his dark curls freshly washed and brushed neatly. Noosh longed to run her fingers through them.

Stop it. You're hardly in any condition to think about sex. She realized Ally was speaking to her and dragged her attention back to her boss. Ally was hiding a smile, obviously having noticed her preoccupation. "Sorry, Ally, I missed that."

"You'll be sitting in on this interview today, Noosh."

Oh, god damn it. She could barely stand the tension between them as it was, and to have to sit by him for the next couple of hours...

Even worse, once they got in the small studio, Ally managed to sit Noosh beside Christo, where she could feel his body heat, breath in his scent of fresh linen and spice. It drove her senses wild and she struggled to maintain her composure. Just before the interview began, Christo looked around at her, and she met his gaze, feeling something shift in the air. She could see he was nervous, and weirdly, she sensed he was looking to her for confidence. She gave him a small smile and a nod, and she saw his shoulders relax. It was such a small moment, but it made her feel... How did she feel? Flattered? Happy? She couldn't tell.

Christo made for an honest, interesting interview. He told Ally about his plans to go into the bespoke furniture business, discussed the stark change of direction, and when Ally questioned him on his father's business, he was honest and forthright.

"I don't pretend that I don't know what my father's business is, and yes, for a long time I took his money and turned a blind eye. From now on…I'm going to try and make up for that. For a lot of things."

Ally nodded. "Do you regret anything?"

Christo was silent for a long time. "Yes, one thing. One thing I regret very much…but it has nothing to do with my father."

Noosh felt a jolt – he was obviously talking about their tryst now…but was he regretting making love to her, or what happened afterward?

WHETHER BY ACCIDENT or by design, Ally bore Bertie off to talk to him after the interview, and Christo was left alone with Noosh. God, he'd forgotten how beautiful she was, how sweet. For a few minutes, they stared at each other then he smiled at her. "Hi."

"Hi." Her voice was wary but soft. He wanted to touch her so badly, stroke her face the way she had his, tell her he was sorry. Instead, he touched the arm of her wheelchair.

"What happened?"

Noosh looked away from his gaze. "An accident."

"I'm sorry."

Noosh gave a strange laugh. "Me too."

Another long silence. "Noosh…that's an unusual name."

"It's short for Anoushka."

"I like it."

She met his gaze, and all he wanted to do was kiss that sweet mouth of hers, hold her in his arms. Christo felt his blood pumping hard through his entire body, his cock twitching, reacting to her. He reached out and stroked her cheek. "Noosh…"

"As I say, Bertie, I'd be most grateful if you would think about it."

Christo dropped his hand as they heard Ally and Bertie return, and Noosh, her face red, looked away from him. Ally and Bertie finished talking about whatever they were talking about, and Christo was saying goodbye.

Noosh shook his hand and he bent down to kiss her cheek. So close to her he could barely stand it, but then goodbyes were said, and he was back in the car with Bertie, feeling bereft now that he was out of her company.

Bertie shot him an amused glance. "I see you were quite taken with the lovely Noosh."

Christo said nothing but gave him a look. After a moment, Bertie's mouth dropped open, having made the connection. "No. *No way. That's* the girl from the club?"

Christo nodded. "She wasn't in a wheelchair then...something happened to her. An accident she said, but...I had the feeling there was more to it."

"But she's the one?"

Christo sighed. "Yes, she's the one."

Ally didn't mention Christo again until they were at home that evening scarfing down pizza. She studied Noosh, who could feel the questions looming. "So, I take it you've met Christofalo Montecito before?"

Noosh sighed. "I have."

"When? Because it seems like, well, the tension between you was pretty smoldering. You sleep with him?"

"Ally."

"Come on, give me details," Ally was grinning. "The man is gorgeous and clearly into you. How come you're not dating him?"

"Because how we met... It wasn't like that – and he wasn't the same man we met today. And besides, I have been occupied with other things. Like almost being murdered, for example."

Ally's smile faded. "Of course, darling, I didn't forget." She put down her slice of pizza. "Listen, Seth and I were talking…I'm sure our listeners would love to hear about how 'Sarah' is doing now."

Noosh chewed her food thoughtfully. "I'm not sure I'm cut out to be on the air," she said slowly. "I've been doing a lot of thinking since the shooting. Maybe my future lies with being your researcher – your best researcher, obviously." She grinned, but Ally didn't smile.

"Anoushka Taylor, you were born for this job. Hell, I've been grooming you for my job since that first day. I've never met anyone with such raw talent, curiosity, and tenaciousness. Cards on the table, Noosh – you're scared."

Noosh swallowed her pizza. "Yes," she said honestly. "I am. I'm scared as soon as I wake up in the morning that whoever tried to kill me will finish the job. I'm scared that everything I've ever worked for is out of reach because of it."

Ally got up and wrapped her arms around her young friend. "Nothing is gone, baby girl. And we'll keep on pushing the police to find out who hurt you. It's okay to be scared, just don't let it rule you."

Noosh wondered if that went for how she felt about Christo Montecito as well. Later, when she was in bed, she couldn't help recalling the way he looked at her, remember his body heat as he sat next to her, maddening her senses with his fresh, clean scent. The way he'd touched her face just before they'd been interrupted. There was an intimacy between them, it seemed, and Noosh wanted to hold on to it, cradle it because it seemed so fragile and yet so right.

Part of her wished she could call him right now and talk, that there was something more between them, that they actually knew each other better so she could reach out. She would give anything to be in his arms right now.

You're being ridiculous, painting him as your knight in shining armor, especially after the way he treated you. But she indulged in the fantasy a little more anyway, thinking back to when his big, thick cock was inside her and his mouth, god, his sexy, soft lips, were on hers.

She groaned and rolled over, pushing away the thoughts. Her back throbbed with pain, and she used that to distract her from Christo, finally falling asleep just before midnight.

WHEN SHE WOKE, all thoughts of Christo vanished when she heard the news that Destry Papps was now his party's official Presidential candidate.

CHAPTER SEVEN

Destry walked off of the stage, the convention crowd still cheering wildly. He grinned to himself and then patted his assistant's arm. "Gerry, they love me."

"They certainly do, Senator." Gervais 'Gerry' Noll grinned at his boss. Ambitious but kind, Gerry had been with the Senator for years, through everything, through the divorce, and Destry's fling with Anoushka Taylor. Gerry and Noosh had become friends, but since the split – or rather, Anoushka's escape – Destry knew Gerry hadn't seen her.

He'd kept the bad stuff from Gerry all this time – he didn't want his closet advisor and probable Chief of Staff, should Destry win the election, to know about his poor treatment of the young girl, or of the attempt on her life.

When Destry discovered Noosh had survived the shooting – barely – he'd panicked. Would she go to the police? There was no way she could prove it was him, after all. Was he stupid to have done the deed himself? No. There was no way anyone could prove it was him, and besides...he wouldn't give up the memory of that night for anything.

. . .

Telling his staff he was headed for an early night, he'd instead sneaked out of his house and into the rental car his contact had procured for him. He'd driven the near four hours to get to her apartment, then broke in easily and waited. When she'd come home, he'd watched her for a while from inside her closet, then when she had fallen asleep, walked to her couch and gazed down at her.

So beautiful...with her long dark hair clouded around her head, her blankets kicked off in the late fall heat, and her top riding up to show the most delectable expanse of midriff. Destry had felt his cock harden. He couldn't risk fucking her and leaving DNA...he'd said her name, hoping she would wake, hoping she would realize she was being murdered...

When she opened her eyes, he grinned to himself, leveling the gun at her belly and firing point blank at her. Noosh had gasped in shock, in agony as the bullet tore into her soft skin and blood began to gush from the wound. Her breathing quickly became labored, but Destry could not tear himself away just yet. He knew he should put a bullet in her pretty head, but he couldn't bring himself to do it, couldn't ruin all that beauty. Instead, he pressed the muzzle against her navel and shot her twice more, her beautiful body jerking from the impact. So much blood. Noosh lost unconsciousness quickly, and Destry knew she couldn't survive the terrible injuries he had inflicted on her.

As he left her to die, he bent down and kissed her mouth, just once, quickly. "I told you I'd kill you if you ever left me, Anoushka."

But she *had* survived. Some nosy neighbor had seen him leave her apartment – thankfully, he had been masked – and called 911. As he drove back to Washington, he scanned the local news for any mention.

Only a few days later did he catch something on the internet. A news report buried in the pages of *The New York Times*.

A YOUNG BRITISH-INDIAN woman working in New York was shot by an intruder in her home in Queens Wednesday evening. The young woman, named locally as Sarah Marsh, was asleep at the time – police say there was no robbery involved and the victim remains in critical condition at a city hospital.

SARAH MARSH? So that's the name you gave yourself to escape me, Destry thought, but it irked him that she had lived, even if she was in critical condition. This is what comes of not using a professional, of making it personal. He should have had his guy kill her, he knew, but then again...

Since the shooting, he had stayed far away from her. His star was rising in the political world, and any scandal was out of the question if he wanted the big job. That Noosh hadn't told the police about him...well, he could see why she hadn't. Who would believe her? Even her parents, who hated him with a passion and who must have guessed it had been him, had said nothing to the British press either, and Destry knew Noosh must have forbidden it.

Destry was deep in thought. When he was President – and he knew he *would* be, come November – then he could make sure she was silenced forever. But any whiff of controversy now... no. He'd let her think he wouldn't try again. Let her think she was safe. Then he'd take it all away, like she'd done to him.

I'll make you suffer, Anoushka. Make the most of the time you have left, my beautiful girl...

. . .

Noosh saw the note on her desk as she wheeled herself into the office the next morning. "It came with these," Liam said, following her in. In his hand he held a vast bouquet of dusky pink peonies. Noosh took them from him.

"God, they're beautiful."

"Like yourself," Liam said matter-of-factly. "If I weren't totally gay, I would so turn for you, Nooshy."

Noosh giggled. She and Liam had always flirted with each other, safe in the knowledge that both of them liked men. "You're such a slut," she teased him, and he grinned. He made no move to leave her alone.

"Come on, open the card, I want to know who they are from."

Noosh rolled her eyes and picked up the envelope. It was expensive paper, heavy, the color of thick cream, and the writing was flowing and confident. *Noosh...*

She caught a faint hint of fresh linen coming off the paper, and her heart began to beat faster. She pulled out the letter inside.

Christo had written only a few words, but they made her head spin.

Lovely Noosh,

I cannot begin to tell you my happiness at seeing you again. I have wanted to apologize for my appalling behavior that night for months, and now it doesn't seem enough to say I'm sorry.

My one regret in life is ever letting you go that night. Can you forgive me?

Please, if you would like, please call me.

For my part, I cannot stop thinking about you.

. . .

Yours always,
 Christofalo Montecito

HER KNEES SHOOK, her legs felt weak. He was so formal, almost old-fashioned. *I cannot stop thinking about you. Nor I you,* she thought and grinned to herself.

"Well?"

She had forgotten Liam was in the room. She smiled at him. "From Mr. Montecito, thanking me for looking after him and Mr. Franklin-Hart yesterday. That was sweet of him."

Liam grinned. "I knew it. I knew some rich mukety-muck would take one look at you and want to sweep you off your feet. And he's dreamy, too."

"*Dreamy*?" Noosh hooted as Liam rolled his eyes. "What are you, six-years-old?"

"So cynical. Okay then, he's very fuckable, is that better?"

"Much."

Liam hopped onto her desk and studied her. "You should get on that."

For a second, Noosh wondered how Liam would react if she told him she had already 'gotten on that.' No. That was her secret, hers and Christo's.

"Did he ask you to call him? I bet he did."

"Mind your own beeswax."

"Huh?"

"Never mind."

AFTER THAT, Noosh couldn't concentrate on anything else. She kept re-reading the note, feeling like a lovesick schoolgirl, but still, she couldn't bring herself to pick up the phone. What the hell would she say?

One decision she did make was to get rid of the wheelchair, no matter what Ally said. Noosh had brought her cane in with her today, and although her back was painful, it felt good to work her muscles, which were almost atrophying from lack of use. She made sure she walked everywhere today and told herself it wasn't just because she felt like she needed to get things…going. Working. Just in case she needed to expend some extra energy…maybe…hopefully…

It was five p.m. when Liam called up from reception. "Honey, there's a delivery for you, but the guy says you need to sign for it personally."

"God, does he look like a process server?"

"No, sweets. Can you come down?"

"Be right there."

Noosh took the elevator – she wasn't confident enough with stairs yet – and hobbled out to the reception. Liam was nowhere to be seen. She glanced around then heard a voice behind her.

"I'm sorry, I made him say that."

She turned to see Christo smiling at her. God, that smile – boyish and warm all at once. He stepped towards her. "I knew you wouldn't call, you see, and so I thought I'd give you the option of telling me to leave you alone in person."

He was close now, and Noosh gazed up at him. "Do you want me to leave you alone, Noosh?"

She shook her head, and he smiled. She wobbled, her legs shaking, and he slid his hands onto her waist, steadying her, pulling her into his hard body to balance her. He stroked her face. "I hate that you got hurt."

"No biggie." Her voice was gravelly, but all she could think of was how nice it was to be in his arms. She couldn't stop staring at his handsome face, his eyes, so soft and full of sweetness. He's looking at *me* like that, she marveled, and then a second later, as he bent his head and brushed his lips against hers, she gave an involuntary moan of desire.

"That," he said in a whisper, "that right there is how *you* make *me* feel."

He kissed her again, his lips firmer this time, his tongue sweeping into her mouth to caress hers, his fingers tangling in her long hair. "God, Noosh...*Noosh*..."

She wanted him to touch her everywhere as he whispered her name over and over, but then she remembered they were still in the very public reception of her building. Ruefully, she broke away, smiling up at him. "Maybe we should go somewhere less, um, open."

Christo grinned. "That sounds promising. How about I take you to dinner?"

"I would love that. Let me just get my bag."

"No need." Liam suddenly appeared out of nowhere, clearly having been spying on them. He grinned unashamedly at them and handed Noosh her bag. "Here you go, sweets, I thought you might need this. Ally says have a good night, by the way."

Noosh gave him a mock-scowl. "All of this seems very...planned."

Christo laughed. "Don't blame Liam, blame me. I'm afraid I've had my spies out for a couple of days – and Liam is remarkably easy to bribe."

Noosh gaped at them both for a moment, then laughed. Who the hell cared? "Well, then you'd better buy me a *really* good dinner, Montecito."

"Warning, she can out-eat a water buffalo," Liam ducked away from Noosh's slap. Christo grinned and offered Noosh his hand.

"Shall we?"

If you want to continue reading this story, you can get your copy from your favorite vendor by searching for the title:

No Promises

A Bad Boy Billionaire Romance

You can also find the e-book version by typing this link in your computer's browser:

https://books2read.com/u/m2xL2r

OTHER BOOKS BY THIS AUTHOR

Saving Her Rescuer: A Billionaire & A Virgin Romance

I was just trying to get away from my crazy ex for the weekend when I ended up in a giant pileup on the highway up to Gore Mountain.

https://geni.us/SavingHerRescuer

Sensual Sounds: A Rockstar Ménage

Lust. Lies. Double lives.

The rock and roll industry is full of people who are looking out for themselves and willing to do anything to rise to the top.

https://www.hotandsteamyromance.com/collections/frontpage/products/sensual-sounds-a-rockstar-menage

On the Run: A Secret Baby Romance

Murder. Lies. Fraud. Just another day in the lives of billionaires and women on the run.

https://www.hotandsteamyromance.com/collections/frontpage/products/on-the-run-a-secret-baby-romance

The Dirty Doctor's Touch: A Billionaire Doctor Romance

I am a master. An elitist. I am at the top of my field, and I know what I am doing.

https://www.hotandsteamyromance.com/collections/frontpage/products/the-dirty-doctor-s-touch-a-billionaire-doctor-romance

The Hero She Needs: A Single Daddy Next Door Romance

He's the only man I've ever wanted...

https://www.hotandsteamyromance.com/collections/frontpage/products/the-hero-she-needs-a-single-daddy-next-door-romance

You can find all of my books here:

Hot and Steamy Romance

https://www.hotandsteamyromance.com

ABOUT THE AUTHOR

Mrs. Love writes about smart, sexy women and the hot alpha billionaires who love them. She has found her own happily ever after with her dream husband and adorable 6 and 2 year old kids.
Currently, Michelle is hard at work on the next book in the series, and trying to stay off the Internet.
"Thank you for supporting an indie author. Anything you can do, whether it be writing a review, or even simply telling a fellow reader that you enjoyed this. Thanks

Facebook
facebook.com/HotAndSteamyRomance

Instagram
instagram.com/michellesromance

©Copyright 2020 by Michelle Love - All rights Reserved
In no way is it legal to reproduce, duplicate, or transmit any part of this document in either electronic means or in printed format. Recording of this publication is strictly prohibited and any storage of this document is not allowed unless with written permission from the publisher. All rights are reserved.

Respective authors own all copyrights not held by the publisher.

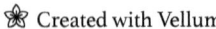 Created with Vellum

www.ingramcontent.com/pod-product-compliance
Lightning Source LLC
LaVergne TN
LVHW011715060526
838200LV00051B/2909